i

ALSO BY KENNARD RAMPHAL

Seeram's Illusions
Teacher Ram's Fascination With Fire
Dilchand Joins The Army
Escape To The Canadian Jungle
Slippery Ochro
(3rd Prize Guyana Prize For Literature: Fiction 2023)

Co-Author with Barbara Verasami and Dwarka Ramphal
Imprints In Life's Journey

RAMLALL'S STRANGE COURTSHIP AND WEDDING
And Other Stories

Kennard Ramphal

MiddleRoad | Publishers

www.middleroadpublishers.ca

"Making Literature see the light of day."

Some of these stories were previously published by MiddleRoad in
Snapshots Of Our Lives Anthology

Library and Archives Canada Cataloguing in Publication
Ramphal, Kennard, author

ISBN 978-1-990765-41-4 (paperback)

Front Cover photo courtesy of
Pexels-weddingphotography-144442 by Viresh
Layout: MiddleRoad Publishers
Design by Kathryn Lagerquist
Kathryn.lagerquist@gmail.com

"Break a vase, and the love that reassembles the fragments is stronger than that love which took its symmetry for granted when it was whole."

—Derek Walcott—

(1930-2017) Nobel Prize in Literature

DEDICATION

This book is dedicated to all the people who touched my life with their love, laughter, and inspiration.

ACKNOWLEDGMENTS

My heartfelt thanks to Ken Puddicombe, owner of Middleroad Publishers, for going through numerous edits of my anecdotes. Thanks to the members of the Carican writers' group, Dr. Harry Persaud, Dr. Roop Misir, Dr. Rosetta Khalideen, and Dr. Frank Mohan for their encouragement and feedback. Ken Puddicombe is also part of this group.

My wife, Orna, has always been a part of my writing, and has endured long periods of isolation from me as I struggled with some passages. I thank her. Thanks to my children, Savita, Yogita and Rajendra, and my sons-in-law, Max Naraine and Simon Eberlie for their constant support.

I thank my brother, Dr. Dwarka Ramphal and my sister, Barbara Verasami, who have read many drafts of my writing and have never tired of giving me feedback.

Many thanks to Barb Scott, Gowkarran Sukhdeo and Michael Laframboise who have demonstrated more confidence in my writing ability than I deserve.

Table of Contents

INTRODUCTION

There has been a plethora of post-colonial successful Indo-Guyanese literature emerging from the diaspora over the past three decades. And the works of Dr. Kennard Ramphal is one of such. At a close look, a literary analyst might find three main elements contributing to this emergence.

First, these writers are baby boomers, born after the war, and grew up, surviving in post-war poverty and under the harsh tutorage of parenthood that was intimately knowledgeable of indentureship. The kind of parenthood who wanted to vicariously escape, through their children, the poverty, drudgery, and discrimination imposed equally by colonial powers and the Christian church, by insisting their children be educated in the very disciplines of their oppressors.

Secondly, these writers suffered a similar trauma that their parents and grandparents suffered. They endured history all over again for nearly three decades under the Burnham dictatorship.

Thirdly, these writers managed to escape both the physical and intellectual prisons of their homeland, and successfully re-establishing in the metropolitan countries, well equipped and prepared by the training and mentorship received from peers, parents and professors. But unfortunately, they were only half-heartedly content, living in semi-exile in a second diaspora, while dreaming, yearning and crying "by the rivers of Babylon" to return, at least in spirit, to an umbilical home, the indelible image of a home that once was, but now non-existent.

In *Ramlall's Strange Courtship And Other Stories*, as in his previous publications, Ramphal closely follows the tradition of established writers Lamming, Walcott, Naipaul, Selvon in Caribbean literature that provides a powerful platform for Post-Colonial Caribbean literature and anthropological studies, maintaining the importance of Caribbean literatures through traditional anecdotal (sometimes humorous) themes of innocence, exile and return to motherland, resistance and endurance, engagement and alienation, and indomitable self-determination. The reader will applaud, cry and even laugh, like Caribbean writers—at themselves.

Ramphal, standing tall as other Caribbean literary stalwarts, is eminently qualified to produce in the above genre, having passed through both the colonial and post-colonial gauntlets.

He was born and grew up in the rustic, agrarian recluse of Canals Polder, once noted for its unique vernacular, cultural traditions, and ethnic harmony. His illustrious career started out as a pupil teacher at the Wales Canadian Mission school in 1957 whence he rose to Senior Master before switching career and joining the Guyana Defence Force. In the newly formed Guyana Army, he reached the rank of Captain and later was appointed Aide de Camp to Guyana's first President. Upon migration to Canada, he returned to teaching, earned his doctorate, and was a provincial education officer in Ontario.

This anthology of stories compiled, and colloquially aptly entitled, is an interesting autobiographical digest of micro stories and encounters of the author.

The young reader today will find that these stories allegorically provide a moral compass and the inimitable footprints for young people today to study, learn and take example from. The imagery that these stories present are worthy of preservation, as they equally reflect the life's accomplishments of the writer. They will empathize with the history, the privations, and accomplishments of their fore parents.

These stories are therefore the cave petrography, indelibly carved on the walls of time and historically and anthropologically links the reader of present generation to those of the past.

Gokarran Sukhdeo BS., MA.
Author and Literary Analyst
Awarded: Guyana Prize for Literature, 1998.

PART 1

BACK HOME STORIES

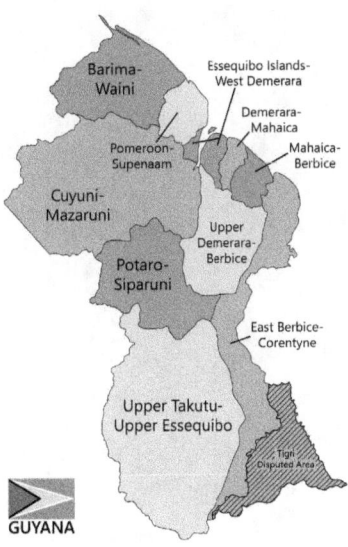

1 THE MORNING I PLAYED DEAD

"*I* told you not to cut grass from Balgobin land," my father scolded me, as his leather belt met my twelve-year-old bottom on a sunny Friday afternoon. He had just returned from Georgetown, where he went to buy supplies for our grocery store, and had stopped at Manbahal rum shop to *tek a few* with the chauffeur, Baba, and some of the other passengers.

When he called me from the vegetable garden where I was watering the vegetables, I noticed that his face was bright red. Daddy's face was always flushed when he drank, but it was much more flushed than usual. At that time, I thought that it was because he drank too much, but I later learned that the cause was a dangerous mix of alcohol and anger.

"Where you cut grass from?" he had asked me, his voice quivering.

I immediately stiffened, because he had repeatedly told me not to cut grass from Balgobin's land. I was trying to decide whether I should lie, but remembered the patch of grass on Balgobin's land would clearly show that some of it was neatly cut with a grass knife. Besides, our black and white cow was still eating the grass, and a person didn't have to be Sherlock Holmes to figure where the grass came from.

I could not determine whether Daddy was angered or frustrated by my silence, but when he repeated the question, his voice was quite a few decibels louder. I felt obliged to answer, albeit evasively.

"Balgobin got long, long grass on his land, and he don't have no cow," I stammered.

"But I tell you over and over again not to cut grass from that man land."

I nodded in acknowledgement, but remained quiet.

1

"When people don't hear, they got to feel," he pronounced. "Go and bring my broad leather," he ordered.

Daddy was referring to an extra broad leather belt he used to wear with one pair of trousers. He could use the belt only on that pair of trousers—the loops on his other trousers being too narrow for it to pass through, and lately, he had resorted to using it as a disciplinary device. I reluctantly went to the bedroom which he and Ma shared, retrieved the belt, and meekly gave it to him.

Daddy was usually a kind man, except when his senses were dulled by alcohol or anger and the sharp pain the leather belt caused on my bottom was the result of both. I did not shout or cry. Daddy never punished any of his children in the yard because, as he frequently emphasized, "Our business is we own," and I was determined not to cry and alert any of our neighbors that I was being punished.

One of my chores every afternoon was to cut a bundle of grass for our cow. We could not allow the cow to roam free, because of the danger of it going into one of our neighbors' properties and destroying their vegetable gardens, or the cassava and plantain plants in their farm. The bundle of grass every afternoon was to ensure that it got enough to eat when I brought it in its pen for the night. Lately, I had encountered some problems in locating grass long enough to cut with our grass knife and I remembered the lush grass on Balgobin's land

Balgobin does not have a cow, or sheep, or goats, I had rationalized. *Why can't I cut grass from his land? The grass is tall and green, and I can cut a bundle very quickly.*

After I was punished, I acknowledged to myself that I should not have ventured on Balgobin's land, but I felt that I did not deserve the pain and the humiliation inflicted on me by my father. I firmly believed that I was a good son. Every morning, when it was my turn, because my brother, Jai, and I took turns to care of the cow, I dutifully took the cow out of the pen and tethered it in a spot where there was enough grass for it to graze on. Then I cleaned the pen, and threw the dung in a heap where it was composted before being used as manure for our small, but lush vegetable garden. I then watered the lettuce, bora, boulangers and other vegetables in the garden, using water from the rain barrel by the side of the house. After that, I showered, ate breakfast, and headed out to school on school-days, where I was considered an excellent student, who almost always placed first in class. I had brooded an entire summer holiday, when Ramesh Mangal, who was a close friend of mine, beat me by two marks and placed first, relegating me to second place.

I knew my parents loved me and I was deeply hurt, physically and emotionally, that my father had punished me so brutally for what I considered a minor infraction.

Earlier in the afternoon, Daddy, dressed in his *going out clothes,* with his new Wilson hat and leather shoes, was walking home from Manbahal's rum shop, staggering slightly, when Balgobin accosted him as soon as he turned into our yard. Balgobin lived two house lots away and apparently sat on his front steps and waited for my father to come home. He was wearing a dirty khaki trousers and a T-shirt whose color could not be determined because of the layers of dust and mud. An old, floppy Wilson hat, ventilated with moth-created holes, graced his head. The entire village of Canal Number 2 was aware that Balgobin always wore this hat because he was quite bald, although he was still in his forties.

When he first started wearing the hat, his acquaintances would playfully take off his hat when they greeted him, allowing anyone who was nearby to see the reflection of the sun on his shining bald head. Frustrated and humiliated, he let it be known that he would slap anybody who dared to take off his hat in future. This threat successfully restrained his friends, and his hat remained on his head.

"I tell you to tell your son not to cut grass from my land," he had told my father. "The long grass *full his eye*[1] and he cut the grass I been saving for Balram. You know that he is my wife cousin, and they give me milk every morning. I tell them that I gon keep the grass for

---

[1] Made him greedy

them to cut. You want to keep cow, grow your own grass."

Balgobin had been staring at Daddy angrily and had not even waited for a response when he had finished his tirade, but turned and stalked off to his home after admonishing my father, who was left angry and speechless.

I envied my two brothers, Kumar and Jai—with whom I shared a bed, the ability to turn and twist as they tried to fall asleep, because the welts in my bottom allowed me to sleep only on my tummy. As my bottom blazed, I wracked my brain to come up with ways to make my father feel sorry for punishing me harshly. Sometime during the night, between sleep and wake, the answer came to me. *I will play dead. That would teach Daddy a lesson. He will be sorry when he sees me lying here and thinking that I am dead.*

In the morning, I did not get up with my two brothers. I knew that it was Jai's turn to look after the cow that morning and I slowed down my breathing, and wondered how long it would take someone to look in and see me in the death posture. I wanted to pee, but not so badly that it made me think of abandoning my plan.

To my surprise, I could hear everybody in the household going about his or her tasks as if everything was normal. Ma was cooking in the kitchen, and I could hear Daddy hammering something in the yard. The sounds of my two brothers gargling as they brushed their teeth and rinsed their mouth reached me clearly, but I was determined to stick to my plan.

If I play dead long enough, they have to notice, I told myself, even as my bladder expanded to almost uncontrollable proportions.

I lay still and took shallow breaths, so that my abdomen did not rise and fall with my breathing, hoping that someone would look in and think that I was dead. The minutes passed slowly and I listened intently, hoping to hear somebody come up the steps and look into the bedroom.

Instead, I heard my eldest brother, Kumar shout, "Ma, pass another roti."

"And give me some more bora," Jai requested. By then, my thighs felt damp and my stomach was rumbling, but I maintained my resolve. "Ma, you better give me some roti too," Jai said.

I wondered if they were doing this for my benefit! Did they *know* what I was up to? I was confident that I could bear the hunger for a while longer, but my expanding bladder was becoming a catalyst for weakening my resolve. There were more than just a few drops of liquid on my thighs by this time. I crossed my legs as I endeavored to stop the flow of liquid, but when I heard the sound of the water running as my mother washed the dishes in the sink, I could wait no longer.

I grimaced as I got up, rushed out of the bedroom and out the back door while unbuttoning the fly of my pajamas. I barely made it to the nearest orange tree, leaned against it, and relieved my grateful bladder. My father, somewhat sober by then, was hammering some nails on the gate of the garden fence, and immediately approached me.

"Balgobin insult me yesterday before I could go into me own house. And he didn't even give me a chance to explain. That's why I was angry with you. Don't cut grass from he land no more. He can eat the grass himself if he want."

I recognized that that was the closest my father would come to an apology and felt that no answer was required of me, so I kept quiet and listened to the soothing sound of my urine as it bounced off the tree and trickled to the ground.

Daddy, too, was silent and waited until the flow of urine ceased before he continued, "Your mom cook roti and fried bora. Go and eat. But wash your hands first," he added, as he looked down at my hands buttoning my fly.

My mom had already dished out my food when I entered the kitchen, after washing my hands at the rain barrel behind the house. It seemed as if everybody's eyes were on me, as I ate like a person who had come back from the dead.

2 PLAYING COW

"*I* can't find the ball," Jairam shouted to Seegol.

The two friends were playing *One tip-two tip*, a variation of cricket on the deserted road in front of Jairam's house on a Saturday afternoon. There were only a few cars in the village and whenever a vehicle approached, they removed their makeshift gear—a garbage can at one end which served as the wicket, and an upturned rusty bucket to mark the bowler's spot.

One-tip-two-tip is a game in which you have to run when you hit the ball two times. It was a popular game when only two or three players were available, because batters could be out more easily than in regular games when batters could *blot* the ball indefinitely.

Jairam, tall and thin, but with broad shoulders was twelve years old, while chubby Seegol, the same age, was short for his age, and his chubbiness made him look even shorter. Jairam wore a blue T-shirt, which was two sizes too large for him, while Seegol sported a white one, which was torn under both arms. Both were hatless and barefoot.

The two had been friends since they started walking together to *Playing Class*² in the one primary school in the village. When they were younger, they played marbles, but graduated to cricket when they got older. Instead of the standard *cork ball*,³ which was used in professional cricket, they played with a *sponge ball*, which was cheaper and safer. Their parents had forbidden them to play with a regular cricket ball, since Basil, an older boy from sixth standard, was hit on the head by a cricket ball and suffered a concussion—according to the doctors at the Public Hospital in Georgetown.

Basil continued to suffer from headaches, so most of the younger boys played exclusively with the softer sponge balls after his accident.

---

² Kindergarten
³ Regular cricket ball, which is hard

Jairam and Seegol often played with some other boys who lived in the area, but on that particular day, none of the boys was available.

Earlier, Jairam had bowled a delivery to Seegol and the ball bounced just before it reached the batter, giving him an opportunity to hit it some distance away in a clump of bushes littered with fallen leaves. After running the length of the makeshift cricket pitch, Seegol joined Jairam in the futile search for the ball, which was their last one. After nearly an hour, they were tired and frustrated—their shirts wet with sweat. A sponge ball cost eighty-five cents at Inderdai's store, and neither of them had money to buy another one. Both friends wondered what they should do in the fading late afternoon light and the limited time they had left.

"The ball done lost," Seegol observed. "Tomorrow, we can search for it again, but it too early for me to go home. Wha' we gon do?"

Jairam scratched his head, furiously thinking of something else he could do with his friend. Then he remembered how fascinated he was by the sound their cow made after it was branded by their father the previous day. He had tried to imitate the sounds, but acknowledged that he was unable to, and he admired Seegol's ability to imitate not only other people's speech, but also the sounds made by animals, including various birds. He remembered that the brand was still lying outside the cow shed on the ashes of the fire his father had lit.

"Let we play cow," he told his friend.

"Wha' you mean?" Seegol replied, "A cow just eat grass all day. Me mother cook good dahl and roti, and you want me to eat grass."

"Yesterday, me father brand our cow, and it make a funny sound. Like this! *Maaahaaa!* —No, I can't do it."

"I bet I can," Seegol boasted. "Remember when I stutter just like Teacher Sugrim. Dhanraj was pissing near cricket pitch, and when I say *D…D…Dhanraj, you got n..n..n..no s..s..shame,* he cut he piss, and nearly shit he pants?"

Jairam laughed loudly as he remembered the incident. Even

Dhanraj, who was the target, had laughed along with the others. Although Jairam admired Seegol's ability to mimic the sounds of animals, he doubted whether his friend could imitate the sound of a cow after it was branded.

"I bet you can't holler like a cow when people brand it," he challenged.

"I can make any sound that I want. God give me that power," Seegol boasted, as he stood straighter and put his hands in his pockets.

"All right! Me father left the brand near we cow pen. Leh[4] we go and I gon[5] press it against you backside and leh we see if you can holler like our cow when it get brand."

The two friends went to the cow pen, where Jairam saw his father's brand lying at the top of some burnt wood. Seeram, proud to show off his skill, got down on all fours, while Jairam grabbed the cold iron, and pressed it against his haunches.

Jairam expected Seegol to make some sounds, but his friend was strangely quiet.

"What happen? Cat got yuh tongue?" he asked his friend.

"I didn't feel nothing."

"You didn't feel the iron because you got yuh pants on."

Seegol accepted his friends explanation, looked around, and seeing nobody around, dropped his pants and Jairam pressed the brand against his haunch.

"Meeeeee!" Seegol screamed. "The iron cold like dog nose."

"Cow don't go *Meeee*. You can talk like some people, and make sounds like some animals, but you can't holler like a cow when people brand it."

Seegol angrily replied, "What do you mean? Listen to this." Seegol made sounds like a kiskadee.

---

[4] Let
[5] Am going to

Even though Jairam knew that it was his friend who made the sound, it sounded so real that he found himself looking up in the trees, searching for a kiskadee. Of course, he didn't see any, and told his friend, "You hear kiskadee making *kiss-ka deee* sound many time. How many time you hear cow make sound when people brand it?"

"You right! I hear the sound cow make when they get brand one or two time. But you know me? Lemme think about it and tomorrow you gon see. I gon holler just like cow. I gon come about two o'clock."

By then, it was quite dark, and Seegol knew that it was time to go home, so he reluctantly parted from his friend. As he walked hesitantly to his home four doors away, he racked his brains to recollect the sound a cow made when it was being branded. Then he remembered that about two months earlier, he was among a group of boys who were looking on when Heera branded his cow and Seegol tried desperately to duplicate the sounds it made. He played the sounds repeatedly in his mind, until he was sure that he could mimic it.

God gave me the power to copy any sound animal and people make, he reminded himself. *Tomorrow, I gon show Seeram that I got that power.*

To increase his confidence, he practiced the sound quietly that night before he went to bed and was still practicing if just before he fell asleep.

The following morning, as soon as he woke up and before he got out of bed, Seegol started to practice the sounds again, and as he walked into the kitchen, Seegol was confident that Jairam would be impressed by his God-given talent.

I gon show Jairam, he said to himself. *He know me fuh so long, and he still don't believe that I can make any sound that I want to make.*

As he enjoyed his breakfast of roti and fried bora, with coffee, he found himself anxiously awaiting the opportunity to show Jairam that he had underestimated his friend's ability. Seegol ensured that he practiced making the sound at regular intervals and the morning passed slowly for him. He regretted that he told Jairam that he would meet him at 2:00, and wished that he had made the arrangements to go earlier in the day, but forced himself to be patient and rationalized that it would give him more time to practice.

At a quarter to two, Seegol set off to Jairam at a fast pace. He was wearing his khaki short pants and an old blue shirt, which he wore when he went to the farm to help his parents. The sun was shining brightly and the day was very hot, as Seegol confidently walked towards Jairam's house.

Jairam had spent the morning picking coffee beans with his mother and the girls she had hired. Although he enjoyed being with the girls, who pampered him and frequently told him how handsome he looked, he remembered his appointment with Seegol, and left to meet his friend.

When he was about one hundred yards from his house, Jairam saw Seegol walking across the bridge spanning the four-foot drain in front of his house, and noticed that Seegol was so anxious to show off his skill that he was practically running.

"I got it down now," Seegol shouted when his friend was about twenty yards away. "Leh we try it right away," as he headed to the cow pen.

Jairam, also anxious to discover whether his friend had learnt to imitate a cow as it was being branded, left his water bottle and his cutlass on the steps of his house and went directly to the cow shed, where Seegol, had already dropped his pants and was crouching on all fours. As Jairam approached the cow pen, he noticed that the branding iron was on a pile of wood and ashes and that some smoke was rising from the ashes. Then he looked at Seegol on all fours, impatiently waiting to show off his God-given talent. He did not want to keep his friend waiting in that position for too long, in the event that somebody would come along and ask all kinds of questions, so he picked up the branding iron and pressed it against Seegol's haunch.

"Owwww!" Seegol shouted, and started jumping up and down. A strange smell assaulted Jairam's nostrils, but he was too focused on Seegol's antics to pay any attention to it.

"Cow don't holler *Owww*," Jairam told Seegol, who jumped into the *four-foot drain* and sat down in the water. "And cow don't do that."

"The brand hot, you *rass*. You burn me."

Jairam's father, hearing Seegol's screams, rushed out of the house, wearing a straw hat and a pair of sleeveless singlets. He had an unfiltered Lighthouse cigarette in his left hand and seemed slightly impatient, because he was getting ready to go and help his wife with the coffee picking.

"Why Seegol hollering?" he asked his son.

"I pretend to brand him so that he can holler like our cow when you brand it, but he say that the iron hot, and it burn him."

"Jaigobin brought his cow for me to brand because he too cheap to pay to get he own brand. So, I brand his cow and left the brand on the fire. I didn't know that you and Seegol stupid enough to play cow and brand one another. Seegol, come out of the *four-foot*[6] and let me see the mark the brand make."

When Seegol came out of the water, he refused to show them the mark the brand had made, although Jairam, who wondered whether it would look the same as it did on cows, pleaded with his friend to drop his pants and show him and his father the mark.

News of the incident spread like wildfire in Canal and everybody, including adults in the village started calling Seegol, *Cow*. The younger children never knew his real name. At first, Seegol was angry when people called him by that name, but he eventually accepted it and laughed when he remembered the incident.

Seegol's friends missed him when they went swimming naked at the conservancy canal on the eastern boundary of Canal No. 2 and he no longer bathed naked at the standpipe in front of his house. Instead, he fetched a bucket of water and bathed in the zinc enclosure that his father had built for his mother and sister.

Eventually, when he got married, even his wife called him, *Cow*,

---

[6] A drain about four feet wide

and years later, when he passed away, two men rode through the village on a bicycle ringing a bell and shouting, "COW DEAD! FUNERAL TOMORROW AT FOUR O'CLOCK!"

3 THE CRICKET MATCH

A single road ran through the Village of Canal No. 2 Polder, where I lived until I was twenty-five. The road was located on the north side of the drainage canal, which gave the village its name, and houses were built on the northern and southern sides of the canal. The lots were about thirty feet wide and a mile long. Many villagers were engaged in subsistence farming and planted coffee, ground provisions and fruit trees on the land behind their houses. Bridges, located at strategic points, provided access to the road for the people living on the southern side of the canal.

The villagers unofficially divided the village into *Top Side,* and *Bottom Side.* Buddy Boy's cake shop was the cultural center of *Bottom Side*—the area east of Manbahal's rum shop, to the conservancy canal, marking the eastern boundary of the village. The community center, located just beside the Perpetua Kawall Canadian Mission School—later renamed Kawall Government School—was the hub of *Top Side,* the area west of Manbahal to Stanleytown, the village west of Canal No. 2.

Canal No. 2 had two cricket teams. Sports Cricket Club played in the cricket field behind the school, located in *Top Side's* turf, while the *Bottom Side's team,* the Cultural Cricket Club played in a cricket field behind Buddy Boy's cake shop.

The rivalry between the Cultural Cricket Club and the Sports Cricket Club was fierce. Whenever they played against each other, there was always a raucous crowd of spectators and very often, disagreements were carried from the pavilion to the rum shops and frequently resulted in fights.

My family lived about half a mile east of Manbahal and were therefore residents of *Bottom Side.* While my two older brothers and I supported the Cultural Cricket Club—it puzzles me up to this day why. Although we lived between two formidable cricket teams and we were not even average cricket players, we naively decided to form our own cricket club.

Behind our house was a grassy patch, located about fifty yards behind the cow pen. Bordered on three sides by coffee trees, it made an ideal miniature cricket field. Cricket beckoned and we eagerly answered. Although our cricket field was much smaller that the regulation field, we knew that our parents would not give us permission to cut down the coffee trees in order to enlarge it. However, the cricket fire in us burned so fiercely that the small cricket field was not a deterrent. We cleared the ground for a cricket pitch in the middle of the patch, cut six relatively straight branches for wickets and carved grooves on the top of the wickets with our pocketknives. Then we put small sticks on the top to act as bails.

My eldest brother, John, had liberated some white chalk from his classroom and we used it to mark the creases. However, we decided that, as professionals, we could not skimp on the bat and ball, so we bought one bat, autographed by Don Bradman, a red Supreme County Game cricket ball with prominent seams to accommodate Andrew's spin bowling, and a pair of pads from Bookers Store in Georgetown.

And we were ready to show the world our cricketing prowess.

A cricket team is made up of at least eleven players. As schoolteachers, we had a certain amount of credibility in the community and we used this to convince eight young men, who were not good enough to play with either the Cultural or the Sports Cricket Clubs, to join us. Because our team consisted of only eleven members, we divided our eleven members into two teams of five, with one person acting as umpire when we played among ourselves.

At that time, cricket mania swept Guyana, including our village—Australia was touring the West Indies and people identified themselves not only with particular teams, but with individual players. To call a batsman, "Rohan Kanhai" was the greatest compliment you could give him. John, Abel and I were not good enough for people to name us after famous players, so we named ourselves.

I called myself Richie Benaud, after the Australian batsman. John called himself Rohan Kanhai. John had a unique style of batting because the movement of his bat was followed by a sweep of his pad, providing double protection, but against the rules of cricket. The great batsman would not have been pleased that someone with John's batting style would be presumptuous enough to adopt his name. Abel, who could hit the wicket two times out of six when he bowled his slow pitch, called himself Garfield Sobers—the renowned all-rounder.

We set our boundaries about twenty feet from the wickets, at the edge of the coffee trees. This meant that a batsman only had to *blot* a ball past the fielders to earn four runs and very often, we would spend over half an hour searching for the ball among the fallen leaves of the coffee trees.

In this situation, who would not feel good about himself after making sixty runs, when Kanhai made a mere fifty? Even individual teams felt good—I remembered our team making two hundred and fifty-one runs in one innings, when the West Indies made a measly two hundred and twenty.

Sooklall, a thin, dark man who was never seen without his straw hat, came through Canal every afternoon with his donkey cart, selling crushed ice, topped with sweet syrup. His arrival was heralded by a sharp, piercing whistle, a welcome sound to many people—in the hot tropical climate, children and adults considered their five cents well spent in exchange for a cup of crushed ice and syrup.

One Tuesday afternoon, John, Abel and I were cooling down after an exhilarating game, when we heard Sooklall's whistle. We rushed to the kitchen to get our cups, snatched five cents each from the cash drawer of parents' grocery store and rushed out the door. Then we slowed down as we saw Sooklall was still three doors away.

While we waited, John decided to remind me and Abel of his batting prowess. "I batted well today," John said, and looked at me and Abel for confirmation.

"I almost hit the wicket three times, but your pad got in the way," Abel retorted.

John looked at his cup and frowned, disappointed that he did not get the recognition he felt he deserved. He was not about to give up, and before he ordered his ice from Sooklall, John told him proudly, "I made ninety-one runs today."

"Ninety-one runs! You are a good batsman," Sooklall responded. "Which cricket team you belong to?"

John hesitated for a few seconds before he responded, "Oh, we haven't named it yet. We want to play other teams." John, of course, knew the two teams in Canal, but was not foolish enough to challenge them.

Sooklall stopped shaving ice for a while and looked at John. "Dem boys in the Stanleytown Cricket Club looking to play another team for practice. You want me to arrange a match for you?"

We had never heard of the Stanleytown Cricket Club, although I rode through Stanleytown every weekday—I had to pass through that village to get to Wales School, where I taught. I was quite certain that they were also not aware of the existence of our cricket club, and we were eager to demonstrate our skills.

"Yes," John eagerly told him. "We can come next week."

"I will tell dem boys, and see if they can play next week," Sooklall responded while he shaved the last cup of ice for us. As he poured the thick syrup in the cup of ice, he told John, "You and your team gon have a good match."

We were on summer holidays and excited by the oncoming match, we found ourselves on our cricket field every day after breakfast with the other team members who could join us. We practiced until the sun got too hot. Then we went inside and did some reading or writing, until it got cooler, and we were able to resume our practice.

"You all stop studying for your exam?" Ma admonished..

Although Ma could read and write quite well in Hindi, she was not literate in English and recognized that education in English was the key to success. She had made all kinds of sacrifices to ensure that her children received a good education, and we followed her advice and studied assiduously. She must have wondered why we were neglecting our studies and focusing on cricket.

"The exam not until next June," John replied. "Plenty of time to study."

"Summer holiday is the only time all of you can be together," she observed. "You can help each other study."

"You never knew that you have three sons who are great cricket players," John bragged. "We have our own cricket team now. We named it John's Cricket Club."

It was the first time Abel and I had heard the name of our cricket club, but we accepted it—we often found it useless to argue with our eldest brother.

Ma gave us an indulgent smile and went about her business, after advising us, "All right! Play your cricket, but study too. Is education make you become teachers, not cricket."

Normally, we would buy *crush ice* two or three times a week, but we found ourselves waiting for Sooklall every day after he promised to arrange the match. On the Monday of the following week, Sooklall found John, Abel and myself anxiously waiting for him, each of us with a cup in one hand, and five cents in the other.

As he shaved the ice for us, Sooklall addressed John, who had nominated himself captain of the team. "Dem boys got the pitch smooth like a billiard table for you. You guys gon come on Sunday?"

"Sunday is good," John told him. "We gon come to start at eleven o'clock."

"Australia and the West Indies start at eleven o'clock. I gon tell them boys to expect you at eleven."

John then remembered that our cricket club owned only a bat and ball and a pair of pads. "We just formed our club," he told Sooklall. "We don't have much gear. Dem boys got cricket gear?"

"Yes, you can borrow their gear," Sooklall reassured us. "Just don't let them wait for you and you don't show up."

John squared his shoulders and held his right-hand shoulder high, with his palm facing outwards. "My word is my bond. We gon come at about ten, so that we can start at eleven."

As Sooklall's cart rolled away, we puffed out our chests and strutted away, savoring our shaved-ice and syrup.

John, Abel, I, and the other team members intensified our practice, and we set out on Sunday with our one bat, one ball, a pair of pads, and high hopes. When our team, dressed in a motley array of shirts and trousers, arrived at the cricket field behind Stanleytown Elementary School, we met the members of the opposing team, all dressed in regulation white outfit, with only two of them wearing floppy cricket hats.

As I looked at the cricket field and compared it to ours, my heart sank. The regulation length pitch seemed much too long, and the entire field appeared gargantuan. One glance at the other members who looked apprehensively at the grounds and at the players, confirmed that they felt the same way.

After the usual pleasantries, John and the other captain, Edmund Manifold, a tall six-footer who taught in Stanleytown School, and the umpire, John Mansfield, the headmaster of the same school, went to the cricket pitch for the toss. John Mansfield tossed a penny in the air, and John confidently called, *Heads*! The penny fell on *Tails*, and Stanleytown Cricket Team elected to bat first.

John selected me as the opening bowler. He was the wicket keeper; Abel was in the fine slip and the other members of the team were allotted their respective positions. I was accustomed to bowling on a much smaller cricket pitch, and as expected, I dropped well short of the wicket on the leg side. The batter waited for the ball to bounce and hit it for a six. Undaunted, I bowled the second pitch, which was way off the wicket to the leg side of the batsman, who was merciful, and hit it only for a four. I gave up one more six, and two fours in that over, and was relieved when it was concluded.

John assigned me to keep square slip while he selected Bayo, who worked in the sugar estate at Wales Estate, to bowl. Bayo was short, but bulky, and was able to bowl quite fast on our small cricket pitch. However, he was obviously as disoriented as I was and dropped the ball in the middle of the cricket pitch. The batter seemed almost bored as he waited for the ball, which bounced two times before it reached him, giving him enough time to adopt a favorable stance, and hit it for a six. All of Bayo's deliveries dropped well short of the wicket, and he gave up two fours and three singles in the over. When I looked at his underarm, I noticed that his shirt was torn, obviously in his effort to bowl on what seemed an over-sized pitch.

I was surprised when John approached me after my disastrous performance, and offered a strategy for the next over, "Hit the batter if you can't hit the wicket," he advised.

I aimed the first delivery at the pad of the batter, who hit the ball which ricocheted off his pad and bounced to the wicket. When I saw the bails tumbling and the umpire raising his hand, I was flushed with success, and aimed all my deliveries to the batter's pad. The strategy was no longer successful, though, and my deliveries were hit either for a four or a six.

Stanleytown was accumulating runs at an alarming rate, but we were able to get a second out when Andrew delivered a slow pitch to the off side, and the batter nicked the ball. John was able to hold on to it.

Stanleytown *declared*[7] when they were ninety-one for two, and it was our turn to bat.

John and I were the opening batsmen, and John faced the first delivery of the fast bowler, a huge player with rippling biceps. John confidently tried the *bat and pad* technique and there was a loud appeal from the bowler as the ball resounded against his pad, which was directly in front of the wicket. When the umpire pointed to the sky with his index finger, John gave him a perplexed look, because nobody would dare to call him out when he played with us. He stood his ground and looked around defiantly, but eventually recognized the futility of any objection and reluctantly made his way to the shaded area serving as a pavilion behind the school.

The next batter, Sunkand, survived two deliveries, simply because he did not swing the bat and the ball bounced an inch or two off the top of the wickets. He was not so lucky on the third delivery and the ball picked off the bails so neatly that the stumps

---

[7] Decided not to bat any more, although all their team members did not bat

remained upright. The bowler appealed and the umpire put up his hand. When Sunkand looked back and saw that the wickets were undisturbed, he could not understand what was happening and refused to leave the wicket until the fielder from the fine-slip retrieved the bails, went to Sunkand, and opening his hands, revealed the bails. Two outs and only four deliveries in the first over.

Ramadhin, our cousin, who lived opposite the school, and therefore was in Sports Club turf, but whom we coerced into joining our team, went to the wicket. A loud shout went up from our team as he managed to blot the ball back to the bowler. Although no run was scored, he showed us that we could at least defend the wicket against this team. My hopes of Ramadhin scoring a run on the last delivery of the over, so that I would not have to bat, went in the way of the bails flying in the dust. However, Ramadhin returned to the pavilion a hero, because he was the only batsman who managed to establish contact with the ball so far.

As I looked at the fast-bowler getting ready for his delivery, I remembered our friendly cricket pitch, and just as I was comparing it to the gigantic monster of the field in which we were playing, the bowler delivered. It all happened so quickly that I did not have an opportunity to move my bat, and the stumps went tumbling. John Mansfield knew me, and I felt that he would have liked to give me a break. Had it been an *LBW*[8], or even a nicked ball, he could have shaken his head for a "No," but there was no denying an *out* when my stumps were all scattered behind the crease.

Instead of putting his hand up for an out, however, he turned to Edgar Manifold, who was fielding in the fine slip, and told him, "Give him another at bat."

Edgar Manifold was not going to argue with his headmaster and nodded to the bowler, who took the ball and went to the spot he had designated as the starting point for his approach.

I was determined to make contact as the bowler released the ball. And I did! The ball rose about ten feet in the air and was deftly caught by the fielder on the offside. Again, the umpire had no choice

---

[8] Leg Before Wicket: when the batsman either deliberately or unintentionally blocked the ball which would surely have hit the wicket.

but to call me out. I half expected John Mansfield to say again, "Give him another bat," but he did not and I remained at the wicket until he came and gently led me off the field.

"You are a good teacher," he consoled.

The remainder of the team did not fare much better, although we did manage to score nine runs, four of them from *byes*, when the wicket keeper missed the ball and it went all the way to the boundary.

Edgar Manifold wanted to give us *two-for-one*[9] and sent us in to bat a second time. Once again, John selected the two of us as the opening batsmen, but remembering the humiliation he suffered in his previous at-bat, he chose me to face the opening bowler. As I looked at the huge bowler rubbing the ball on the leg of his white trousers, he returned my gaze and smiled.

I thought, *If a cat can smile as it is looking at a mouse, that is the smile it will give.*

He ran and delivered his pitch and I was lucky that I froze. It appeared that the bowler was too confident, or perhaps the ball simply slipped from his fingers, because it was way off on the leg side. The wicker-keeper made a desperate lunge for it, but could not reach it, and it sped all the way to the boundary for four runs.

Although I did not do anything, I heard, "Go, Deo, Go!" And I raised my bat like a hero.

The freezing technique worked again for the following delivery when the ball bounced a foot above the wickets. On the third delivery, before I could raise my bat, all three of my stumps tumbled to the ground. This time, I was determined to save my dignity, and did not wait for the umpire to say, "Give him another at bat," but walked off the field with my head held high.

The remainder of the team batted slightly better than they did in the first innings, when we scored fifteen runs, all out.

Edgar Manifold turned to his team and asked, "Should we give

---

[9] When one team bats two times and still cannot beat the score of the opposing team which batted once

them *Three for one?"*

"Nah!" the wicket keeper, who was upset because he did not get an opportunity to bat, exclaimed. "We had enough fun for today."

Members of John's Cricket Club joined two hire cars and went home in silence. On the way home, I gave a great deal of thought to the humiliating defeat we suffered and rationalized that Stanleytown Cricket Club, like John's Cricket Club, was a new club, with Sooklall as its unofficial manager. Sooklall was wise enough not to match the team with a strong team at the beginning, but like the manager of a novice boxer, he matched it with a team which would ensure an easy victory. How he recognized John's Cricket Team as a team which could be easily beaten was anybody's guess.

When we arrived home, although Ma knew we had lost by taking one look at our faces, she asked John, "How the match go?"

John did not answer, perhaps because he wanted to spare Ma the extent of our humiliation. Instead, he turned to me and Abel, "You know how much para-grass we can grow on that piece of land? We won't have to go to other people's land to cut grass for our cow."

Ma consoled us immediately. "The three of you very bright. Look at all the exam you pass."

John stood a bit taller. "Ma, you know that none of we ever failed an exam yet?"

"God bless me to have bright children," Ma said, as she lowered her head, and clasped her hands.

"They say that the more you put into Shakespeare, the more you get out of him. Leh we read *Merchant of Venice* again," John told me and Abel, as he went to the pile of books on the table.

Neither Abel nor I replied. We were too humiliated to concentrate on Shakespeare, as we tried to forget our first and last cricket match.

4 ABEL AND THE DUCK

On an overcast Saturday afternoon in our rural village of Canal Number Two Polder, my elder brother, Abel and I were studying for our teachers' exams for most of the day.

I was not surprised when, at about four o'clock, Abel closed *The History of the British Empire* and turned to me, his brown eyes unwavering, as if he was still concentrating on the events in British history. Looking at his intense facial features, I understood why he had the reputation for having an almost photographic memory, which I envied, especially when I tried to recall dates and events in history, or the names of characters.

Lean and wiry, Abel was eighteen months older than I, but we grew up as if we were twins, and wrote the Pupil Teachers' Appointment Examination, and almost all the other teachers' examinations, together. There was always an air of friendly competition between us in our studies and I attempted to compensate for my inferior memory by studying assiduously. Very often, I would be at the table long after Abel had gone to bed.

Abel told me, "This is nice duck weather. Ducks always come to the mango trees just by the edge of that swamp behind our farm. We studied enough for today. Let's go and see if can shoot a Muscovy duck or two."

I needed no prompting. After teaching the whole week and studying all Saturday, I was feeling listless and bored and had to frequently force myself to concentrate.

"Let's go!" I replied. "We can continue studying tomorrow, when we are fresh."

We felt satisfied that we put in almost a full day of study and after we changed into our *Back-dam clothes* we wore to work in the farm, we put on our worn-out sneakers and set out with our father's sixteen-bore shotgun and six cartridges. We envied the people who could walk barefoot, because the thick calluses on the soles of their feet protected their feet from thorns. As teachers we were required to wear shoes and the soles of our feet were quite soft, making it unthinkable for us to go to the farm, or to the jungle without any footwear.

Ma, who was our unofficial supervisor of study time, apparently also felt that we had done enough for the day, and watched us indulgently as we got ready. I felt that she was pleased that we chose to go duck hunting, instead of us indulging in our usual Saturday evening activity—drinking at Prag's rum shop with our friends.

The sun was partially hidden by clouds and the air was laden with moisture, but Abel and I were not concerned about getting wet. On the contrary, brimmed with the bravado of youth, we welcomed the rain as we walked along the path between the coffee trees laden with red berries. We wanted to show anybody who saw us that, although we were teachers, we were as rough and tough as the other youths in the village.

"Ducks like to feed at dusk," Abel reminded me, "and they like wet weather. Today looks like a good day for them."

"The number five cartridges we have are good for ducks," I observed. "But this time when we shoot the duck, let's go right away and find it while it's still stunned from the fall. Remember the time when we shot a duck as it was flying, and we spent so much time congratulating each other, that when we went to pick the duck up, we found that it was only wounded, and it hid so well in the swamp that we couldn't find it and we had to go home empty-handed?"

Abel laughed as he remembered the incident. "You were the one who wanted me to congratulate you on your good shot, otherwise we would have gotten the duck," he reminded me.

I jumped at the opportunity to show off the Latin phrase I had learnt earlier that week, and with my hand on my chest, I told him, "Mea Culpa!"

Abel smiled indulgently. Although we were extremely upset at that time for not getting the duck, we found that we could subsequently laugh at the incident, and continued to talk about our foolishness as we walked towards the end of our farm.

After about an hour's hike, we hid among a clump of bushes near a mango tree and waited. Behind the tree was a large expanse of swamp. Although ducks and other edible birds frequented the swamp, few people ventured there, because it was believed that it was the habitat of camoudies and alligators

After concealing ourselves, we waited for about an hour. The few drops of rain which began to fall increased our hopes, but although we saw ducks flying and landing in the swamp, none was attracted to the mango tree. Only about a quarter of the sun was visible on the western horizon and without articulating it, we both thought that we were waiting in vain, when we saw a lone Muscovy duck flying towards the tree. It circled two times, as if it was trying to make up its mind, and then landed on one of the top branches. Although it was partially covered by the branches, we could see its outline quite clearly. Abel's hand was steady as he cocked the shotgun, rested it on the branch of small tree and took careful aim. My elder brother took pride that he was a good shot, and I had as much, if not more, confidence in him as he had in himself.

We were both aware of the mechanics of the shotgun. When you cock the hammer, a mechanism pulls the firing pin back. Then when you pull the trigger, the pin is propelled forward with force, and strikes the detonator of the cartridge. If you have a bird-shot-cartridge, many small lead pellets will be guided through the barrel of the gun and the pellets will hit the target. If the target happens to be a duck on a tree, the law of gravity dictates that the duck will fall to the ground.

There was a loud boom as Abel pulled the trigger and I expected to see the duck fall to the ground, but was disappointed to see it flying away, apparently unharmed.

"Let's go and look under the tree for it," Abel said.

"But I saw it fly away," I told him. "You must have barely missed it," I added, consolingly.

"That must be another duck," Abel stated emphatically. "I don't miss. It has to be under the tree."

He walked purposely towards the mango tree and I reluctantly followed him thinking, *When he doesn't find the duck, he will accept the fact that he missed.*

We searched for half an hour, and as can be expected, we found no duck. Abel was not discouraged, but continued searching persistently, while I kept him company and waited for him to finally admit that he missed. Eventually, it got quite dark, and even darker under the mango tree.

Although I was accustomed to my brother's tenacity, I was gradually losing patience and I gently put my hand on Abel's shoulder. "The duck flew away, Abel. It was on one of the top branches of the tree, and it was a difficult shot. We will try again next weekend."

"It has to be under the tree," Abel insisted, while looking at me resolutely. "I rested the gun of a small branch, so the gun wouldn't shake. I don't miss," he emphasized, as he continued to part the undergrowth.

When it became so dark that it was impossible to continue searching, Abel reluctantly decided to return home. We had walked along the path many times before, so the lack of visibility was not a problem.

"We will have better luck next time," I consoled Abel.

I expected that he would finally admit that he missed the duck, but Abel still had the determined look on his face as he told me in a confident voice, "We will bring Rex and Brutus tomorrow morning to search for it. It can't hide from the dogs."

5 SAM, PEARL AND SHAKESPEARE

In 1961, T*welfth Night*, was required reading for English Language and Literature in the GCE—*General Certificate of Education, Ordinary Level[10]*. I made my way to the Ministry of Education in Georgetown to register to write this exam, because success in five subjects, including English and Mathematics, was the equivalent of a Third-Class Teacher's Certificate. I had already written the *Third-Class Exam*, but I was not sure whether I would be successful, and I regarded the G.C.E. as a sort of insurance. This was my first exposure to Shakespeare in print, and *Twelfth Night* still holds a treasured spot in my memory because of several reasons.

My eldest brother, Sam, who liked to display his knowledge of English to flatter the young women he knew, collaborated with me in reading and interpreting this beautiful Shakespearean comedy.

We were living in colonial British Guiana at that time, and Sam was totally enamoured of the English. He and I taught at the elementary school in Wales Estate, and he was always admiring the White managers as they sat regally in their land rovers driven by one of the locals. A fan of Western movies, he was also enthralled by the White overseers as they rode on horseback on their way to the sugar cane fields.

Sam, like many people in Guyana and most colonial countries, tried his best to emulate our colonial masters who lived in a compound reserved solely for them. The only locals allowed on this hallowed ground were the cooks, gardeners, domestics, and others who served the White overlords.

As a dark-skinned twenty-one-year-old man, with thick, black hair, my eldest brother was far removed from the English as far as appearances were concerned. He attempted to address the most obvious symbol, his skin color, by staying out of the sun for lengthy

---

[10] Grade 12 equivalent in North America.

27

periods, while diligently applying various skin lightening creams and ointments on his face and hands every night. When the applications caused rashes all over his face, while his skin remained dark, he finally accepted the fact that there was nothing he could do about his skin color.

Then there was his hair. Whenever he went to the cinema, located obliquely opposite the school, and saw a show featuring the English or people of European descent, he always admired their blonde hair. There were no beauty salons in Canal, and trips to Georgetown required a great deal of time, so changing his hair colour was not an option. He thought about shaving his head, but decided against it. It was the custom in the Hindu religion that the eldest son, was required to shave his head when a parent died, so doing it while our parents were alive had superstitious and religious implications.

When Sam realized that there was nothing he could do about his skin or hair color, he did the best he could to imitate the English in other ways, within the limitations of the resources and culture of our village.

We all knew that *Afternoon Tea* was an old English custom and every afternoon Sam insisted that we took a break from our studies and went downstairs to "have a cup of tea." He always endeavored to pronounce the words in quotation marks with an English accent.

We were reading *Twelfth Night* and Sam was completely obsessed with Shakespeare's mastery of the English language. As we walked down the stairs leading to the kitchen, he told me, "Man, I wish I can flatter a girl like that. There is no other writer in greater command if the English language than Shakespeare. Look at how Viola sweet-talked Olivia! I wish that I can flatter a girl like that," he mused as we entered the kitchen.

My mother had five sewing apprentices and they vied with each other every afternoon to make tea for us. Whether they wanted a break from their sewing machines, or whether they wanted to be in the company of two relatively good-looking bachelors who were teachers, was anybody's guess.

Pearl had recently joined the four young women in my mom's

sewing class. She was a dark, eighteen-year-old with sparkling eyes and long hair falling loosely down her back. Her oval face sported a perfectly shaped nose and full lips. That day, Pearl chose to wear a skirt and a tight blouse, which accentuated her well-formed body. She was obviously aware of her attractiveness and walked with a flounce, the movement of her breasts under her thin blouse causing a great deal of excitement for many young men, including Sam and myself.

Like most girls in our village, Pearl wore no make-up. Villagers made fun of the few women who put on make-up, and one woman, who had recently married and moved to the village, had applied some *Ponds* powder on her face when she went to pick coffee. She was called *Ponds Powder* by everybody in the village for the rest of her life.

Pearl was the eldest of five siblings and her parents had pulled her out of school as soon as she was old enough to look after her younger siblings. This had enabled her mother to go to Wales Estate and work in the *Weeding Gang.*[11] Her mother had taught her to cook as soon as she was tall enough to reach the fireside made of a mixture of clay and cow-dung and she did a pretty good job of preparing meals for the family, although her father frequently complained that the gravy of the curry was too watery. All that remained in her preparation for marriage was for her to learn to sew. At the time the incidents related in this story occurred, that aspect of her learning was being addressed.

The only treat available to take with our tea was the local equivalent of a cracker, called *salt biscuit* by the villagers, and Sam went directly to my parents' small grocery store to get some crackers and some *Cow and Girl* butter. Pearl left her sewing machine and walked seductively through the kitchen to heat some water on the kerosene stove that we had bought the previous Christmas for Ma. We wanted to save her the trouble of looking for firewood for our home-made fireside every time she had to cook. While Pearl lit the stove and put the water in an aluminum pot, Sam bought a plate of crackers and some butter on a small pate, and placed them on the

---

[11] The group of people was hired to get rid of weeds, around the plantation.

table.

It was a warm day and all the animals around were seeking relief from the heat under the many trees in our yard. There was usually a light breeze which alleviated the heat, but there was none on that day, making the kitchen stifling hot, even with all the windows open. The heat from the stove and the water boiling in an open pot made it warmer for Pearl, who started to perspire freely as she put some tea leaves in the boiling water. After allowing the brew to steep for a few minutes, she strained it, then she added condensed milk and sugar, before pouring the tea in two enamel cups.

Her hips swayed seductively as she walked to our table with a charming smile. As she placed the hot, sweet tea before him, Sam badly wanted to ask her to sit and have some tea with us, but he knew that Ma would have objected. She always spared one of the girls to make tea for us, but Sam guessed correctly that it would make the other girls jealous if we sat down to have tea with one and not the others.

Apparently, Pearl was also reluctant to return to her sewing machine, and stood staring at Sam after she put the cups on the table. As Sam looked at the dark-skinned beauty, rivulets of sweat running down her face, and her blouse soaked under her arm, he racked his brain to find the appropriate language to impress her. Then the light bulb went on and he remembered *Twelfth Night.* He stretched his right hand out and paused for a few minutes, as he tried to summon an English accent. Then, as if he were on stage, he recited, "Tis beauty truly blent/Whose red and white nature's own sweet and cunning hand laid on."

At this stage, Sam paused and looked at me for confirmation. When I nodded, he continued, "Lady, you are the cruel'st she alive/If you will lead these graces to the grave/And leave the world no copy."

Pearl froze like a deer caught in the headlights of a vehicle and looked at John in bewilderment. I noticed that she was sweating even more than before and I could almost hear her brain torturing itself as it tried in vain to make sense of what she heard. She knew that it was not Creole and was certain that it was not Standard English, because she had listened to our radio many times, and most of the programs were in English.

When she finally could not figure out what John was saying and what language he was speaking, she gave vent to her frustration. "Talk English you *rass*,[12]" she exhorted, as she exited the kitchen and joined the other trainees in the sewing area.

[12] Local mild swear word

6 HOW I TRAUMATIZED MY COUSIN

My mother was born in the rice farming village of Windsor Forest, on the west coast of Demerara and lived there until she got married and moved in with my father's family in Canal Number 2, located on the west bank of the Demerara River. Most of the residents of Canal No. 2 were unaware that the land was originally swamp which was reclaimed by the Dutch, who colonized Guyana for some time, until the British took over the country. People who lived in Canal were engaged in subsistence coffee and provision farming, and many worked on the sugar estate in Wales.

International travel was unknown to us and our holiday travels were limited to visiting Windsor Forest, where we spent time with our cousins, Ramesh and Vishnu. I was four years older than Ramesh, who was, and still is one of my favorite cousins. He was the son of my mother's brother, *Coot Mamoo*, a kind and helpful man who always endeavored to make our holidays in Windsor Forest enjoyable.

One activity I really enjoyed with Coot Mamoo was going by the seaside to catch crabs, which we would either curry and eat with roti or rice, or put in a coconut soup. My mother's family had several coconut trees on their property, so the supply of coconuts was almost unlimited. I still remember the time, not so fondly, when we caught crabs and cooked a coconut soup with them. All through the night, there was a line-up for the latrine, because of the diarrhea caused by eating too much coconut.

My grandfather, who sported a large handlebar moustache, and whom everybody called *Major,* always laughed loudly whenever he saw us, obviously enjoying the visits of his daughter's children.

Just as we enjoyed our trips to Windsor Forest, Ramesh and Vishnu relished their visits to Canal Number 2 and we looked forward to their visits as much as we looked forward to visiting them. The fact that there were not enough beds for all of us—we had to sleep on rice bags (jute bags) on the floor—did not detract from the joy we felt when our cousins visited. We were as close to our *Windsor Forest cousins* as we were with our siblings and Ma was as happy, if not happier than we were, when her brother's children visited.

The times we spent together were golden moments of pleasure.

In the summer of my sixteenth year, everybody was overjoyed when we saw Ram, suitcase in hand, walking across the bridge spanning the canal to our home. The single road in our village was on the north side of the drainage canal and several bridges provided access to the houses on the south side, where we lived.

Ram was tall for his age—almost as tall as I was—and sported a perpetual smile on his face. He demonstrated a deep regard for the well-being of others that was far advanced for his age. I really liked and admired these qualities and endeavored to earn his complete trust.

During Ram's visits to Canal, everybody tried to make his stay as enjoyable as possible and we picked fruits that were in season, either from our farm, or our neighbors' farms. Most afternoons were spent swimming in the sweet, black water of the conservancy canal, about a mile east of our home.

My father owned one of the few shotguns in our village and the meat he provided by hunting *acouris,*[13] ducks, and *anakwahs*[14] was a welcome addition to our meals of mostly rice or roti, and some sort of curried vegetables. When I turned fifteen, my father had trusted me enough to allow me to hunt with our shotgun and I endeavored to earn his trust by contributing a few acouris, ducks, or anakwahs to the family diet.

One afternoon, Dhanraj, a friend of about my age, and who enjoyed telling jokes and playing pranks, visited me, and we decided to take Ram hunting in the forest south of our home. Ram was very excited, and told his aunt, "We gon bring home an accouri, or a duck Aunty."

---

13 A type of rabbit
14 A tasty bird, somewhat like the partridge

Ma's face beamed with pleasure as she looked at her nephew.

With high hopes, we set out on the path between the coffee trees, keeping our eyes peeled for anakwahs nesting among the thick branches of the trees. We saw none of the tasty birds and emerged from our coffee farm to enter the jungle behind the farm, named *Hampa Bush* by the villagers. We walked as quietly as we could, hoping to see an accouri between the bushes, or a duck or a *powis*,[15] in the trees. Ram was the most vigilant of the three of us.

After walking for about half an hour, an accouri ran across our path but it was so fast that it disappeared in the bushes before I could bring the shotgun up.

"Did you see the accouri, Deo? Why didn't you shoot it?" Ram asked me

"It was too fast. It just ran quickly across the path."

"Look how fast Audi Murphy is. Audi Murphy woulda got it."

"Audi Murphy is in the movie. This not the movie. This is real life."

Ram remained silent, but his disappointment about my not being fast enough to shoot the accouri was evident, and I felt inadequate.

I attempted to console my cousin. "We will see another one. Hampa Bush got plenty accouri."

We continued walking and peering between the thick undergrowth and up in the trees, but none of us saw anything. Once we heard a rustling of dried leaves. There was obviously something going to cross the path in front of us and I cocked the shotgun and waited quietly until I could see the game. We were all disappointed and slightly afraid when we saw a twelve-foot camoudie sliding across the path. Everybody froze, and I raised my shotgun and aimed at the camoudie, deciding whether I should shoot it, but decided against it. The noise of gunfire might scare off any game.

After the camoudie passed, we spent another half an hour walking and earnestly hoping to find some game. I badly wanted to

---

[15] A large edible bird, called "bush turkey" by the villagers.

show my cousin how good a shot I was, but it was not our day, and I became frustrated and disappointed when it began to get dark. I had to accept the fact that we would go home empty handed.

Up to this day, I cannot explain why I decided to play a trick on my beloved cousin. In retrospect, I think that I was trying to compensate for my lack of success in finding some sort of game and my failure to understand the long-term consequences of my actions.

"I think that we're lost," I said.

Dhanraj caught on immediately. "We have to sleep in the bush," he said, looking at Ram, who remained stoically quiet, and was probably confident that his cousin would protect him.

When I saw that our ploy was thus far effective, I decided to increase the dose. "We have to sleep in the trees," I added. "But we have to sleep in different trees, so that if a tiger should come, it will eat only one of us. It will probably choose the smallest one."

Ram, understandably, became very scared, and started to tremble and cry uncontrollably. I immediately relented.

"We were just joking, Ram. I know where we are, and we'll go straight home."

However, he kept on crying intermittently all the way home and was still sobbing when we reached, although I constantly tried to reassure him. He was quiet as he showered, and he was quiet when he changed his clothes, while I was so ashamed of my behavior that I was fervently hoping he did not tell Ma of the prank we played on him.

Ma asked Ram as we sat down to dinner, "Ram, why you so quiet? You miss your daddy?" Ram's mom had passed on some years earlier.

I froze as Ram started to speak. "No Aunty! I okay." Then he added, "I sorry that we didn't get any accouri, Aunty."

Ma thought that Ram was quiet because we didn't bring home any game. "Don't worry about that, Ram. We gon kill a fowl tomorrow, so we can have curry chicken and roti."

Ram did not answer, but sat on the low seat, which we called a *pirha*, and ate his dinner of rice, curried potatoes and eggs in silence.

The following morning, everything appeared to be normal, with Ram a bit more talkative than the previous evening, and I felt more relaxed about my thoughtless prank. My cousin spent a few more days before returning to Windsor Forest, but did not mention the hunting trip.

I forgot all about the incident and thanked my lucky stars that no further harm was done.

In adult life, Ram joined the Guyana Police Force and I enlisted in the Guyana Defence Force, where we both had successful careers. Years later, the politics of Guyana encouraged both of us to leave Guyana, Ram to the United States, and I to Toronto. After a few years of struggle, we were relatively successful in our adopted countries and settled down with our respected families.

One Christmas, more than fifty years after the incident, there was a reunion of myself, my brother Dwarka and his wife, Rita, in Ram's house in Miami, Florida. Dwarka and Rita had travelled from North Carolina to be with us.

Apart from the pleasure of meeting my brother, his wife, and my cousin, it was very refreshing for me to escape from a minus twelve-degree weather in Toronto to a plus twenty-two-degree climate in Florida. We were relaxing on the very comfortable porch at the back of Ram's house, enjoying a third drink of fifteen-year-old El Dorado, and smoking Cohiba cigars, when Ram turned to me and said, earnestly, "Bud, you were my best cousin, but I still remember how you traumatized me."

I racked my brains to remember when I caused harm to Ram, but could not come up with anything. "What do you mean, Ram? I always looked out for you. I cannot remember ever harming you in any way."

"Remember when you and Dhanraj took me hunting? And you told me that we were lost, and that we would have to sleep in trees? And you emphasized that we would have to sleep in different trees, so that if a tiger comes, it would eat only one of us? And it would probably choose the smallest one. That thing is still traumatizing me. When I went home to Windsor Forest, I had dreams of a tiger eating me. Even in adult life, I still wake up at nights and think about sleeping in a tree, and tiger coming to eat me."

"Oh my God! I remember now. That was so long ago. And we were just joking, Ram."

"You were joking, but I trusted you, and believed everything you said. I really thought that we were lost, that we had to sleep in trees, and that a tiger might come and eat one of us."

"I am so sorry Ram. I did not know that you would be so traumatized by the incident."

I poured a large drink of El Dorado to help me numb my pain.

"The incident was meant as a harmless prank, Ram. It never occurred to me that it would have caused such long-lasting trauma. I was only sixteen years old at that time, but I should have known better. I am really sorry, Ram."

At that time, in Canada, I was an anti-racist consultant, and I had emphasized during the workshops I facilitated that actions and words have lasting consequences. I had also reminded participants that, when you say or do something, it's not the intent that matters. It's the impact that the words and actions have on others.

I have used the incident involving my cousin in subsequent workshops to illustrate the above points. It revealed to me the harmful and long-term effects of my foolish actions in my salad days and I have learnt a valuable lesson.

7 I KNOW I PASSED

My elder brother's first name was Jewarhirlall, but everybody, except the teachers in our school, called him *Jai*. He was sixteen years old, while I was fourteen. Jai was in the class above me in Perpetua Kawall Canadian Mission School, but we ended up in the same *Pupil Teachers' Appointment* (P.T.A.) class of seven students in our school in Canal No. 2.

In the year Jai was eligible to write the P.T.A. exam, the headmaster, Mr. J.G. Boodhoo, did not have a P.T.A. class. There were many conjectures as to the reason he chose to do this. My father thought that Mr. Boodhoo did not like Jai because my brother was a very stubborn and opinionated individual, and often questioned his teachers when they presented facts and opinions. Often, Jai was correct—to the displeasure of his teachers.

For example, our teacher in Fifth Standard, Mr. Singh, took immense pleasure in pointing out how clever a judge was, when three brothers went to him and asked him for help in dividing their father's estate. Their father had seventeen sheep and gave his eldest son half of the sheep, his second son one third, and the youngest son one ninth. The sons disputed bitterly as to how they could divide the seventeen sheep.

Mr. Singh told the class that the judge simply added one of his own sheep to the seventeen making the total eighteen, and gave the eldest son nine sheep, the second son six sheep, the youngest two, and then took back his own sheep. Then he saw Jai writing in his *exercise book*.

"Jewarhirlall, why are you writing while I am talking?" he shouted.

Jai stood up. "Sir, the father did not divide his entire estate. One half, one third, and one ninth do not equal the whole. It is only 17 over 18."

Mr. Singh froze for a few moments, before realizing the truth of

Jai's statements. "You're too smart for your own good," he said with a scowl, before continuing his lesson.

**

Students who were successful in the P.T.A. exam were eligible to become *pupil teachers*—literally teachers who were learning to teach under the guidance of more experienced teachers. For many students, teaching provided a way out of working in the sugar estate, either in the office, or cutting the sugar cane stalks and loading them into punts in trenches. The other alternative was to work in the coffee and ground provision farms, for which Canal No. 2 was famous.

Jai's stubbornness may have led to the fact that he was left with few options after he passed the *School Leaving Examination* and received his *Primary School Certificate*. My parents knew that he could not get a teaching job with this certificate and my father was debating whether he should learn tailoring, or to tend the grocery store they owned. Working in the sugar estate was not an option, so Jai remained in limbo until the following year, when I passed the *School Leaving Examination* and Mr. Boodhoo decided to have a P.T.A. class.

My parents had the foresight and wisdom to persuade Jai to return to school and enroll in this class, although it was very unusual for someone to go back after passing the *School Leaving Examination.* I imagine that Jai felt a certain amount of humiliation when he picked up his books, and joined me in my walk to school after a year's absence.

We knew that this exam could make or break us, and we were determined to be successful, and studied assiduously. In fact, we did so well in the class that Mr. Boodhoo often told the remainder of the students, "You watch those two brothers."

On the appointed day, Jai and I travelled to Georgetown to write the crucial exam and after each subject, we anxiously compared our answers. We got the same answers in Arithmetic and although the answers in the other subjects were not as straightforward as those in Arithmetic, Jai was convinced that he did as well as I, if not better.

When we returned home, our eldest brother, John, who was already a teacher, was waiting to grill us on our responses to the exam questions, and he confirmed that we had done well, assuring us that we had passed. We were well aware that the exam was highly competitive, because if the Ministry of Education wanted 200 teachers, only the top 200 candidates "passed." This meant that a candidate could get 79% and still "fail," but we were convinced that we would be among the candidates who were successful.

In previous examinations, the names of successful candidates were published in the daily newspapers, *The Daily Chronicle* and *The Daily Graphic,* but in the year we wrote the exam, for reasons known only to the officials of the Ministry of Education, letters were sent to the headmasters of the schools in which students were successful, asking them to advise students that they were required to attend interviews with officials appointed by Ministry of Education.

On a Tuesday evening, about three months after we had written the exam, we had just finished dinner and Jai and I were upstairs at the table studying, while Ma and Daddy were in the kitchen. It was quite dark, and we could not see beyond the light which our Petromax gas lamp offered, but we were alerted to the presence of a visitor by the barking of Rex and Brutus, our black and white dogs, which did not really attack visitors, but merely served as early warning systems.

When Daddy stepped outside to calm the dogs and welcome the visitor, he was surprised to see Jack Mungal, whom everybody in the village called *Teacher Jack.* Teacher Jack usually took a drink or two with his friends in one of the local rum shops, but did not routinely call on any of the villagers.

Daddy had become friends with Teacher Jack when Teacher Jack was courting a beautiful, slim teacher who was of Chinese background. Teacher Doris was from Rosignol, but was assigned to teach at our school and was boarding with our neighbors, Morris and his wife, who were also of Chinese descent. Eventually, Teacher Jack and Teacher Doris got married, and bought a house about a mile and a half west of the school.

A lanky six-footer and the Deputy Headmaster of our school, Teacher Jack was in the process of dismounting from his bicycle when Daddy greeted him.

"The dogs just bark—they won't bite," Daddy reassured him. "It very dark, Teacher Jack. I hope the headlights of your bicycle working."

"They're working, but I also know the road," Teacher Jack reassured Daddy." He was referring to the one brick road which ran through the village. Villagers knew every pot-hole and every bridge along the road and could navigate their way in the darkest of nights. Teacher Jack leaned his bicycle against one of the posts of the steps, and told Daddy, "I got good news for you, Mr. Ramphal."

Daddy was immediately alert. "Come upstairs, Teacher Jack."

As soon as they were upstairs, before he sat on the chair Daddy had offered, Teacher Jack pulled out a greyish-brown envelope from the pocket of his white shirt. Daddy could see *Ministry of Education* printed on the top left-hand corner of the envelope. Teacher Jack extracted a letter from the envelope, and again Daddy could clearly see the Ministry of Education letterhead, as Teacher Jack passed it to him, while saying, "Deomitr passed the P.T.A. exam. He has to go for an interview with Mr. Slanger Davies, the headmaster of Queen's College, next week Wednesday at eleven o'clock. The interview is at Vreedenhoop Anglican School."

As Daddy started to read the letter, Teacher Jack continued, "I want Deomitr to come to my house tomorrow so that I can prepare him for the interview."

Daddy was reading the letter as Teacher Jack turned to me, and asked a preliminary question, "Deomitr, why do you want to become a teacher?"

My fourteen-year mind was extremely naïve. "Teachers earn a lot of money and get long holidays," I responded.

Teacher Jack laughed, as he looked at me and then at Daddy. "Many people become teachers for that reason, but if you tell them that, you will fail the interview."

He turned to Daddy. "That's why I want Deomitr to come tomorrow, and we will practice some questions that are likely to be asked at the interview

Jai was silent through it all and looked at Teacher Jack

questioningly. Daddy, who had finished reading the letter and was holding it in his hand, asked the question that was on Jai's mind. "Only Deomitr passed, Teacher Jack? What about Jewahirlall? He study *even and straight* with Deomitr for the exam. And he bright, too."

"We got the letter only for Deomitr," Teacher Jack replied noncommittedly. I noticed that he avoided looking at Jai.

Jai did not move from the table, but listened to the conversation with a puzzled look. Meanwhile Ma had come upstairs and was also a silent listener.

Although one of his sons had apparently failed the examination, Daddy wanted to show his appreciation to Teacher Jack for taking the trouble of coming to our house and informing us that I passed.

He told Ma, "Give Deo some money. Let him go to Sedan and buy a bottle of rum."

It was obvious that Ma wanted to say something, but did not know what to say, or how to say it. She went quietly into her bedroom and took a five-dollar note from the roll that she kept in her dresser drawer, and wrestling with her mixed emotions, returned to the company and handed the bill to me. I immediately left for Sedan's rum shop, which was conveniently located three houses away, while Ma found the words to console my puzzled brother.

"Don't worry, Jai! We gon send you back next year to write the exam. You bright. You gon pass next time."

"I can't fail," Jai exclaimed. "I gon go to the interview and tell them I passed."

The following morning, I left to cycle over to Teacher Jack, and Ma picked up my white shirt, to be washed at the standpipe in front of my house. She looked at Jai sadly as he brought the blue shirt that he intended to wear to the interview. The following day, as I was polishing the one pair of black shoes that I owned, Jai sat beside me, and started to polish his brown shoes. And later in the day, when Ma started to iron my shirt and trousers, Jai handed her his shirt and trousers. Ma accepted Jai's clothes with a sad and perplexed look and desperately thought of ways in which she could comfort her son.

On the Tuesday evening before the interview, Jai was as ready as

I was, although Ma and Daddy tried to convince him that Teacher Jack said that only I was selected to attend an interview. When I hung the clothes I planned to wear on the nail behind the door of our bedroom, Ma and Daddy looked sadly at Jai as he selected the clothes which *he* intended to wear. The silence was broken by the barking of Rex and Brutus, and Daddy hurried downstairs to see who was visiting. A few seconds later, we all heard the familiar voice of Teacher Jack.

"Jewarhirlall also passed the exam." Teacher Jack intentionally spoke loudly so that we could hear him clearly upstairs.

Daddy hushed the dogs and ushered Teacher Jack upstairs, where Jai and I looked at each other. Jai was smiling and looked at me as if to say, *I told you I passed.*

As soon as he entered the door, Teacher Jack stretched out his hand. "Congratulations Jewarhirlall! You passed!"

"I knew I passed," Jai simply replied, as he returned to the table.

Teacher Jack sat on one of the chairs around the table and explained to everyone. "The clerks at the Ministry of Education made a mistake, and sent the letter that Jewarhirlall passed and has to attend an interview, to Mr. Sahai, the headmaster of the school in Canal No. 1. Mr. Sahai sent somebody with the letter to me this afternoon. You don't have a lot of time to prepare to prepare for the interview."

 Only then, did he pull the familiar envelope from his shirt pocket, extracted the letter and gave it to Jai, bypassing Daddy this time.

Jai simply said, "Teacher Jack, I know that I passed, and I am prepared." Then he leaned back in his chair folded his arms, and gave Teacher Jack the widest smile I ever saw him give anybody.

Ma, who had come upstairs from the kitchen to join us, had tears in her eyes. Once again, she wanted to say something, but she didn't know what to say, or how to say it.

Daddy practiced a bit more restraint, as he fished a five-dollar bill out of his pocket and handed it to Jai. "Go to Seedan and buy a bottle of rum."

"They got to go to the interview tomorrow," Ma reminded Daddy.

Daddy laughed loudly as he looked at Ma, then at Teacher Jack, and then again at Ma, before he responded, "Jai and Deomitr got interview tomorrow. I don't have no interview. Teacher Jack you got any interview tomorrow?"

Teacher Jack recognized it as a rhetorical question and just looked at Daddy and smiled.

Before he left to go to the rum shop, my elder brother looked at Teacher Jack intensely. "Teacher Jack, I knew that I passed."

Teacher Jack responded with a quizzical look as Jai headed out through the door. I wanted to accompany him, but at some level, I intuited that he wished to be alone, even if it was just for a short while.

Nobody minded when the Daddy and Teacher Jack drank late into the night, even when sounds of their conversation and laughter carried through the entire upper storey, because the walls of the bedrooms did not reach up to the ceiling.

The following day, dressed in our freshly starched and ironed shirts, our trousers with sharp creases, and our highly polished shoes, Jai and I attended our interviews with Mr. Slanger-Davies. I had previously shared the *correct* answers with my brother, and we were successful at the interview. Both of us were hired as pupil teachers, after being baptized in the Christian faith, and changing our names to *Andrew* and *Kennard*.

We did not particularly appreciate the fact that we were required to be baptized—Jai in the Methodist domination and I in the Presbyterian domination—before we became teachers, but I will forever admire my elder bother for his unwavering confidence in himself and his refusal to believe that he failed an examination in which he had done so well.

8 FORGETFUL ABEL

Our entire household was overjoyed when my brother, Sunilall, who was eighteen months older than I, was hired as a pupil teacher in Affiance Methodist School after being baptized by the Methodist minister. The Christian name he had chosen was *Abel*. Before his baptism, we had all called him *Sonny*, an abbreviation of his Hindu name, and we had to mentally struggle to get accustomed to his Christian name. Through an inexplicable process, over time, we addressed him by only by his Christian name. The notable exceptions were Ma and Daddy, who continued to call him, Sonny.

Tall and skinny, Sonny was close friends with our cousin, Deodat, who lived about a mile west of our home, and worked at the sugar estate at Wales. They started experimenting with alcohol and cigarettes at a very young age, when Sonny liberated cigarettes from our grocery store, and met Deodat at our aunt's grocery store and rum shop. There they bought a cheap brand of wine, called *Pak-pak* by the villagers, and the two cousins experienced the thrill and the effects of the alcohol and nicotine, which they enjoyed in a thatched shed behind our aunt's house.

Ma and Daddy were very happy that Sonny got a job as a pupil teacher, but Ma became also simultaneously sad, because it was the first time any of her children had to leave home for more than a week or two at a time.

Affiance was a small village on the Essequibo coast and because we lived in the rural village of Canal No. 2 Polder, on the west bank of the Demerara River, Abel had to ride his bicycle to Vreed-en-hoop, after asking one of the friendly hire-car drivers to take his heavy suitcase and leave it at Choo's cake shop, conveniently located near the train and ferry station. After collecting his suitcase, Abel had to take the train to Parika, then board the ferry across the Essequibo River to Suddie, and finally cycle for five miles to

Affiance.

It required a full day of travel and therefore the only times that Abel was able to visit home was during the Christmas, Easter, and of course the summer holidays. Daddy had arranged for him to board and lodge with one of his friends, Ramroop, for a modest amount of money. Ramroop, who owned a cake shop, lived in a convenient location, about a twenty-minute ride from Affiance Methodist School.

This meant that Abel had to pack all his books and every-day stuff needed for about three months. This posed a constant challenge because Abel's head was always in the clouds. This is a kind way of saying that he was very forgetful.

Ma and Daddy knew of the cigarettes and the *Pak-pak* and frequently debated whether they were the cause of Andrew's forgetfulness. However, they both knew intuitively that Abel was like that by nature.

School was about to start and Abel was naturally extremely excited about his first teaching job. On the second day of September, 1957, a pampered fifteen-year-old, who had never been away from home for any significant length of time, packed his suitcase and asked Ma's first cousin, Budya, a hire car driver, to drop his suitcase to Choo's cake shop. Ma cried as Abel jumped on his Humber bicycle and began his ten-mile ride, on a brick road, to Vreedenhoop, the first leg of his journey to the school where he would start his teaching career.

Three days after Abel left, a postman arrived at our home, leaned his bicycle against the coconut tree in front of our home and handed Ma a telegram. Ma could read and write Hindi fluently, but could not read or write in English, although she understood perfectly when people spoke Standard English, so she passed the telegram to Daddy, who signed for it. Before reading the telegram, he opened the kerosene fridge we kept in our grocery store and took out a bottle of cold Pepsi, which he handed to the sweating postman, who accepted it gratefully. As the postman was drinking the Pepsi, Daddy looked at the telegram.

Ma anxiously said, "What the telegram say?"

Daddy glanced at the telegram and then looked up at Ma. "It is from Sonny. The telegram say, *PLEASE POST RAINCOAT.*" Daddy's face reflected both frustration and amusement. He was frustrated because he knew that he would have to be the one to bicycle to Wales, where the nearest post office was located, and post the raincoat. He was also amused because he and Ma were always joking about how forgetful Abel was.

"Sonny always forgetting something. Now he forget his raincoat, and he asking us to post it," he elaborated. "He and Deodat been to Inderdai yesterday and drink *Pak pak*, or else he mighta remember."

Ma was surprised that Daddy, who always stuttered when he was upset or excited, did not stutter on this occasion. "I sorry that he get a teaching job so far. I don't want rain to wet him and make him catch cold. I gon put the raincoat in a box, and you go to the post office tomorrow and post it."

"I got to waste a whole day to post the raincoat for him."

"They don't have any store in Affiance he can buy a raincoat from," Ma replied soothingly. "You go and post the raincoat. Don't worry about the laborers. I gon go and work with them."

In order to discourage Daddy from complaining further, she immediately left, took a box from our grocery store and folded Abel's mackintosh raincoat. After squeezing the raincoat in the box, Ma sealed it securely with masking tape and wrapped some strong twine around it. She tied the string securely, then turned to Daddy. "You got Ramroop address? You got to write the address on the box."

Daddy went upstairs to the table we used for reading and writing, selected a pen and came down to write Abel's name and Ramroop's address on the brown box. The following morning, Ma went with the laborers to weed the coffee farm, while Daddy jumped on his Humber bicycle and rode the nine miles to Wales Post Office, where he posted the box.

I wish Sonny make sure that he pack everything before he leave. Look how much trouble he give me, he thought as he cycled back home.

As he approached Inderdai's rum shop, Daddy rationalized, *The day spoil already. Lemme make a bad job of it,* and he steered his bicycle into the path leading to her shop. Inderdai was his sister, so he spent some time catching up on family matters before he ordered a quarter bottle of El Dorado rum.

The reader who is familiar with rum shop etiquette will not need any explanation why Daddy invited Bhai Bhai, a close friend of his, to have a drink with him as soon as Bhai Bhai entered the rum shop. He will also understand why other friends who walked into the rum shop would have invited Daddy and Bhai Bhai to have a drink with them. When the bottle from which they were drinking was finished, the reader will understand why Bhai Bhai felt that it was his turn to buy a bottle. Rum shop etiquette would dictate that he buy a large bottle when there were five people at the table. The result was that Daddy, totally inebriated, went home at about one in the morning.

Ma understood that he was frustrated at losing a whole day's work at the farm and didn't say anything when he came home wasted, although she knew that he wouldn't be able to do a full day's work the following day.

As he slid into bed, she asked, "You post the raincoat fuh Sonny?"

"Yes. Then I drop in at Inderdai for a quick quarter. As soon as I pour the first drink, Bhai Bhai walk in, and I say it gon look bad not to invite him for a drink, so I tell him to come and tek a small drink with me. Then Baba and Googol and Sunil come in."

Daddy would have given a detailed account of the night's proceedings, but even in his intoxicated state, he noticed that Ma was already snoring while he was relating the events at the rum shop. Feeling deprived that he did not get an opportunity to tell the entire story, he had no option but to snuggle up to his wife, before falling asleep.

Abel wrote intermittent letters telling us how he was getting on in school, and although we missed him, everybody was happy that he got a teaching job and was doing well. Before we knew it, Christmas holidays loomed and everybody was overjoyed when Abel came home. The trouble Daddy took to post the raincoat was forgotten amid the celebrations and gift giving, until it was time for Abel to return to Affiance. Abel asked Polo, who drove a blue Vauxhall hire car, to take his suitcase to Vreed-en-hoop, and Ma watched sadly as he jumped on his bicycle to start his day-long journey.

On the second day after he left, it was raining and Ma and Daddy were a bit surprised to see a figure approaching our house in a raincoat, because people would not venture out in the rain unless it was very important. As the figure approached, Daddy's face mirrored all kinds of emotions as he recognized the postman who had delivered the earlier telegram. The postman, who was understandably upset at having to come out in that weather, pulled out a waterproof bag from under his coat, extracted a telegram and a receipt, which he handed to Daddy, and pointed to the place where Daddy had to sign. Daddy signed the receipt and handed it back to the postman, who looked at him expectantly, anticipating the offer of another Pepsi. But Daddy was experiencing too many emotions to think about mundane things like Pepsi, so the disappointed postman left. Daddy held the telegram in his hand for a long time, while Ma was anxiously waiting for him to read the contents.

"You gon open it, or what?" she said.

Daddy was still wordless as he looked at Ma, paused for quite a few minutes and shook his head before he opened the telegram. Daddy took one glance at the telegram and then looked at Ma with something between a frown and half smile.

"*PLEASE POST LONG BOOTS,*" he read to her. Both looked at each other wordlessly for quite a few minutes. Daddy looked as if he wanted to say something, but then thought better of it.

Ma, surprised that Daddy did not stutter, broke the silence. "I really sorry for Sonny. We can't blame *Pak-pak* this time, because he and Deodat did not go out last night."

She then placed her hand on Daddy's arm to placate him. "Munny and Dhanraj get teaching jobs close to home. Dhanraj can come home every day, and Munny can come home every Friday. But Sonny teaching so far away."

She looked at Daddy with tears in her eyes as he remained wordless, before she continued. "I gon go and put the long boots in a box so you can post it tomorrow." She then went in our grocery store to select a suitable box, leaving Daddy in a dazed state.

It had rained during the night but although the rain had stopped when Daddy started bicycling to Wales Post Office, the road was very muddy, and Daddy had to stop a number of times to remove mud from between the wheel and the frame of the bicycle. By the time he arrived at the post office, his shoes were full of mud and he ignored the disapproving look the postal worker gave him as he looked at Daddy's shoes when he entered the post office.

After mailing the long boots, Daddy experienced the same difficulties in cycling home again and was tempted to drop in at his sister's rum shop on his way home, but resisted the temptation and went directly home. Out of frustration, he did not go to the coffee farm to assist in weeding, although it was only 1:00 p.m., but went directly to the kitchen, opened the cupboard where he kept a bottle of rum and poured himself a tall drink. Then he went to bed to sleep off his frustration.

Abel wrote the following week to acknowledging his receipt of the long boots, and to inform us of his progress and his intention to stay in Affiance for the Easter holidays, so that he could have more time to study for the Pupil Teachers' First Year Examination in June.

In June, when Abel was about to leave Affiance to write the exams, his headmaster, a kind sixty-year-old man who was near retirement, told him that he did not need to return to school after the exams to teach just a few days before the school closed for the summer break. He indicated that he would give Abel a few days leave so that he could start enjoying the summer holidays early.

We had foreknowledge of Abel's arrival in June when Polo dropped his suitcase off at our home, but there was no time for celebrations when he arrived, sweating on his bicycle, because our exams were on the following day. Abel and I traveled together to Georgetown to write our teachers' exam, and when the results were published in the local newspapers in mid-July, we were happy, but not surprised, to learn that we both had passed.

The summer holidays just flew by and soon it was time for Abel to start packing. "All of you say that I always forget something," he repeatedly told us as he packed to leave for over three months once again. "This time, I will not forget anything," he emphasized as he folded his raincoat, and put it in his suitcase.

Then he put his long boots in a large paper bag, which Daddy had brought from Bookers Stores, and squeezed it in his suitcase. He checked, and double checked that his ties, belts, socks, shirts and trousers were packed in his suitcase. On the day before he was scheduled to leave, however, he made arrangements to meet Deodat, in order to say farewell over some cigarettes and a few sips of *Pak pak*, and came home very happy. On Sunday morning, Abel took his suitcase, went by the side of the road, and hailed Budya's hire car to begin his journey, while the remainder of the family looked on sadly. As expected, Ma was in tears.

This was always a sad time for everybody, including me. My eldest brother left later in the day to go to the East Bank to begin his teaching stint at Providence and I, accustomed to the company of my two eldest brothers, was left sad and alone.

Two days after Abel left, the sky was overcast and a heavy wind caused the branches of the trees to be quite agitated. In fact, the coconut tree in front of our house was swaying so much, Ma and Daddy were afraid that it would fall down. When Ma took her eyes off the coconut tree and looked at Sedan's bridge, which spanned the canal separating our house from the main road, she saw a man in a postal uniform shakily making his way across the narrow bridge.

She did not say anything, but Daddy directed his gaze to the direction in which she was looking and saw the familiar sight of a postman making his way to our house.

"What he forget this time?" Daddy asked Ma.

Ma continued looking at the postman, thinking, *I help him pack his raincoat, his long boots, all his shirts, ties, and socks, his handkerchiefs, everything. What he forget now?*

The postman, still nervous about his ordeal relating to his crossing a narrow bridge while a gale-force wind was blowing, handed over the telegram and the receipt to Daddy who accepted them. Then, anxious to remove himself from the situation, the postman left as soon as Daddy returned the signed receipt to him.

When the postman left, Ma and Daddy looked at each other, neither wanting to break the silence, until, unable to bear the frustration any longer, Daddy opened the telegram with trembling fingers. Ma, who found herself unable to stand, sat on one of the chairs beside her sewing machine, but was anxiously and nervously leaning forward.

Then Daddy started to read the telegram, "PPPLEASSSE PPOSSST BBBICYCLE."

9 ABEL AND WHAT MAKES IT TICK

A bel was five feet, ten inches tall, thin as a broomstick, and tired of people teasing him about his leanness. About two months before summer holidays, his drinking companion, Basil, short and squat, with a massive chest and firm biceps, told him in a voice loud enough for everybody in the rum shop to hear, "Abel, yuh chest and yuh belly the same size."

They were drinking from a bottle of El Dorado rum in Manbahal's rum shop, on a busy Saturday evening and the other two drinking companions, Paltu and Mahadeo, also very muscular, nodded in agreement. The other patrons looked at Abel and smiled.

Although Abel did not respond to Basil's comment, he spent a great deal of time worrying about it, and tried to figure out ways on how to change that particular situation. As luck would have it, he happened to come across an advertisement in *The Sunday Chronicle* the very next day.

BUILD YOUR BODY IN JUST TEN MINUTES A DAY, the advertisement had screamed. A picture beside it showed a handsome and muscular Charles Atlas, proudly displaying his muscles to the world. The blurb explained how Charles Atlas was a ninety-seven-pound weakling, and when some hoodlums kicked sand in his face and in the face of his girlfriend, poor Charles could not stand up to them. He was so traumatized by the incident that he developed and performed several body-building exercises. When the exercises resulted in Charles Atlas being named *THE WORLD'S MOST PERFECTLY DEVELOPED MAN*, he decided to share his secrets with the world for only $49.99.

Abel went to the mirror, took off his shirt, looked at this lean body, and cut out the advertisement from the papers. He carefully completed the form which accompanied the advertisement, and addressed an envelope, using the address conveniently located at the bottom of the form. The following day, he rode to the post office at Wales, about nine miles away, purchased a postal order for $49.99

53

and included it in the envelope which contained the completed form. Then he asked the postal worker for the correct postage to send the letter express mail, bought the stamps and mailed the letter.

It should come in time for the summer holidays, he thought, as he cycled back home. *I gon get Dhanraj to exercise with me. I gon show Basil and dem boys. I gon get a body just like Charles Atlas.*

The package, with a list of prescribed exercises, arrived two weeks before the summer holidays, but and Abel and I waited until we had written our Pupil Teacher's Second Year Examinations before we attempted to follow the instructions outlined in it.

Our exercises included push-ups, using two chairs, and pull-ups on one of the low branches of the orange trees surrounding our house, sit-ups, jumping rope, and other activities, but involved no weights, because Charles Atlas used no weights. Every day, we checked the mirror in vain for any welcome signs of bulging muscles like the ones Charles Atlas displayed.

After two weeks, the only difference we saw, or rather felt, was consistent and nagging pain in our pectoral, arm and leg muscles, and other muscles that we didn't even know we had. Obviously, the course was not working, and Abel began to lose interest. I, of course, lost interest with him.

At the same time that we decided to abandon the Charles Atlas course, our parents were involved in picking coffee berries from our farm and had hired some young women from our village to help.

Abel told me one day as we were studying, "We need to move more. *The Charles Atlas Course* is just ten minutes a day. We need to move the whole day, and exercise all the muscles, instead of sitting at the table reading and writing."

"I agree! We done pass the Pupil Teacher's Second Year Exams, and we don't have another exam until next June."

Two weeks earlier, our names had featured in *The Daily Chronicle*, among the candidates who had passed the *Pupil Teacher's Second Year Examinations*. We had written the examination at the end of June.

"Ma and Daddy picking coffee. To pick coffee, you got to move the whole day, and use a lot of muscles. Leh we go help them."

"You just want to go because Leila going," I teased. "You know that Ma and Daddy hire Leila, Babso and Cecelia, and I know that you *got eye pon* Leila."

"That too! But this Charles Atlas course ain't doing shit, except hurting all my muscles. We need to exercise with natural movements. Tigers don't exercise, and look at how fluid their movements are."

I thought of all the pain I was feeling throughout my body and told Abel, "If you say so. Besides, Ma and Daddy paying people to pick coffee, and we home. Leh we go help them."

Abel announced our decision to Ma that evening as we sat down to a dinner of curried boulangers and potatoes, and roti.

"Dhanraj and me gon come and help you and Daddy pick coffee tomorrow."

Ma, a frail woman with endearing manner, who made numerous sacrifices for her children to receive a sound education and escape the hard life of a laborer, smiled at Abel.

"Good," she told him. "The coffee so ripe that it falling, and we got to pick them up from the ground. But the coffee farm got so much bush that we can't get all the coffee from the ground. You and Dhanraj got to wake up early if you gon come and help."

"All right Ma! Wake me and Dhanraj up."

"Okay! I gon wake you up. You gon help us until we finish picking all the coffee? I notice that you start so many things, but you don't finish them."

"We gon help you pick coffee until you finish picking all the coffee, Ma. We done pass our exam and we on holidays."

"So, you say," Ma replied skeptically.

The following morning, Ma woke us up at 6:00 and after breakfast, we set off with her, Daddy and the three girls she had hired. Ma and Daddy had picked coffee from the trees nearest our house earlier and decided to start the day at the perimeter of our coffee farm. I chuckled when I saw that Abel chose to walk beside Leila, almost touching her.

When we reached the end of our farm, Ma gave each of us a converted flour sack. She had sewn the edges so that it would not unravel. We knew the drill and tied one end of the cloth around our waists, then tucked and secured the loose ends to the one around our waist to create a small bag in the front in which to put the coffee berries. There were baskets, placed along the path in which to empty our bags when they were full.

Between the end of our farm and the end of our property, there was a large patch of land which was half-swamp. The land in Canal No. 2 was *pegasse*, consisting mostly of decaying leaves and plants, making the soil very fertile, but it also made it burn easily. An earlier fire had burnt this patch of land, transforming it into a swamp and making it unsuitable for coffee cultivation.

Abel climbed a tree at the very edge and started to pick the ripe, red coffee berries from a branch. Then his eyes lingered on the burnt piece of land and he started to contemplate.

"All that land going to waste," he said. "We can plant rice on that land. But if nobody else plants rice, birds will eat all of our paddy. We have to encourage all the neighbors to plant rice, so birds will eat a little from each farm, and we will still get enough to make a profit."

In the beginning, Abel was talking to us, but did not notice that we had moved quite far from him as we picked all the berries from the trees near him and moved to other trees. When he continued to plan how to encourage the neighbors, how to prepare the land, how to irrigate it, how to plant and reap the rice, and how to transport the paddy home, he was in fact talking to himself.

Eventually, Abel climbed down from the tree which afforded such an excellent view of the swamp and emptied his pouch containing about fifty berries into a basket. "I am going home," he announced to everybody.

Because he was a volunteer and not a laborer, Ma and Daddy

couldn't object, but as soon as Abel was out of earshot, Daddy made a prediction—loud enough for everyone to hear. "Either the clock or the radio gone."

Daddy was referring to the large wall clock, which my eldest brother, Jonathan, had bought when he had passed his Third-Class Teachers' examination. Clocks and watches were not very prevalent in Canal in those days, and we were so proud of it that we kept our windows open, even when it was raining, so that people walking on the road could see what time it was. Another of our prized possessions was our radio. Radios were also uncommon in Canal at that time, and we accommodated requests by neighbors to turn up the volume up when Radio Demerara played Indian songs in the morning, and made death announcements every night at 9:00.

Daddy made the above prediction because he and Ma had recognized the fact that, in addition to starting many projects and abandoning them as soon as he became interested in another, Abel had an inquisitive mind, and was interested in what made things tick. He would often take things apart, and then discover that he couldn't reassemble them.

On the other hand, I had a tendency to stick with projects even when everything was not going well. In fact, I was known to continue working on projects, even when the results were counter-productive. I guess that my parents were not surprised that I continued picking coffee until the end of the day. Nobody seemed to mind that I was picking from the same tree as Cecelia for most of the time.

At the end of the workday, we loaded the wicker baskets full of red coffee berries into the *corial*,[16] and pulled the boat in the four-foot drain which led straight to our home. Once we were home, we unloaded the berries from the corial and placed them in a heap. Later, we would pass the berries through a grinder to split the pulp, so that they could dry more easily. Daddy would then take the dried coffee berries to *Coffee Baba*, Ma's cousin, who owned one of the two village factories which separated the beans from the pulp.

After we finished unloading the corial, Daddy washed his hands and feet by the rain barrel beside our house, went upstairs, and

---

16 Long, narrow wooden boat

almost whooped joyfully when he saw Abel sitting at the table. Abel had a small screwdriver in his hand, and the clock lay face down on the table, with the hour hand and the minute hand beside it. An assortment of little wheels and different parts of the clock were scattered around it, like planets orbiting the sun. Abel was so engrossed in contemplating the parts of the clock that he did not notice Daddy approaching.

He actually started when Daddy shouted, "Nel! Come up here!"

Ma hurried upstairs. When she reached the head of the stairs, Daddy, who stuttered when he was angry or excited, pointed gleefully at the table told her, "YYYou aalways sssay that I tttalk tthat I wanted to ssay tthat something gon happen, bbut tthis time, I ddidn't. Ttthis time I ttell yyou before. Wwwatch!"

He looked at Abel as if he wanted to hug him.

Ma looked at the dismembered clock with dismay. Then she looked sadly at Abel, who had ceased his contemplation of the clock and had raised his head to acknowledge the presence of our parents.

Abel's grey eyes focused intensely on Ma and Daddy, before he ventured an explanation. "It was slow, and I was going to fix it. Lemme rest a bit, and I gon fix it tonight when we light the Petromax gas lamp."

Ma and Daddy were speechless for a long time before Ma pointed to the scattered parts on the table. "How you gon fix all this?"

Then, with a sigh of resignation, she began to walk away to prepare dinner. However, she stopped at the head of the stairs, and turned to face Abel. "At least, go and cut a bundle of grass for the cow. The clock done gone," as she glanced again at the mutilated clock.

Abel reluctantly got up from the table, but just before he passed through the door, he stopped at the head of the stairs, turned, and looked wistfully at our radio, sitting silently on a shelf above the table.

10 RAMADHIN'S ROOSTER

My cousin Ramadhin, a thin, dark-skinned nineteen-year-old, who worked at Wales Sugar Estate, loved anything on wheels, and considered himself extremely lucky to land a job involving ploughing the sugarcane fields with an estate-owned tractor.

He was a warm and sensitive individual, who created and maintained strong bonds between his friends. Many people tried unsuccessfully to be friends with him, because Ramadhin did not take friendship lightly, and chose his friends very carefully. I considered myself lucky to be chosen as a member of his inner circle, because many relatives did not make the cut.

"I can't choose my relatives, but I can choose my friends," he repeatedly told me."

Ramadhin was very expressive, and after a few drinks, he frequently turned to his friends and loudly proclaimed, "I don't have many friends, but my friends I would die for." And then he never disappointed his listeners, who expected him to quote Shakespeare's lines: "He that is thy friend indeed/He would help thee in thy need/If you sorrow, he would weep/If thou wake, he cannot sleep."

Cousin Ramadhin did not limit his friendship to humans, and had a favorite red rooster which he raised from the moment it popped out of its shell. Over time, the rooster imprinted itself on Ramadhin and a steadfast bond developed between him and the bird.

Whenever Ramadhin sat down to eat, either in the hammock or sitting in one of the wooden chairs designed for the bottom house, the rooster confidently strutted to him and Ramadhin shared his meal, dropping some rice or roti, or curried vegetables on the ground. When Ramadhin and the rooster first developed this relationship, the other chickens tried to approach him and partake of his offerings, but were vigorously shooed away. After a while, they did not even bother to go near our cousin and left him to pamper his favorite rooster.

As the rooster matured, Ramadhin admired its bright red coxcomb, and sometimes he stretched out his hand full of rice and had the rooster literally eating out of his hand.

In the evening, the rooster felt so safe that he slept on the lowest branch of the orange tree which was just outside the kitchen, while the other chickens chose the upper branches.

In spite of repeated objections from my mother, Daddy had bought a brand-new Morris Oxford, affectionately nicknamed, *The Bull*, because it successfully ploughed through the brick and dirt road which ran through the center of our village, even when the rain caused the road to be muddy and full of potholes, and many cars got stuck in the mud.

"You and them boys, gon just take the car to go and drink all over the place," she had told my father.

At sixteen, I was the youngest of *them boys*—my elder brothers being eighteen and twenty.

My father insisted that he and the boys will run the car *private-hire*, meaning that although it would be registered as a private car to save on insurance, we would run it as a *hire-car* and bring in enough money to pay for the purchase and its upkeep. My two older brothers and I were teachers, and my father was a tailor, so running the car as a hire-car on a full-time basis was not possible.

We thoroughly enjoyed the convenience, the prestige and the admiration of the young women our new car offered, and one of our routines every Saturday night was attending *The Plaza*, a cinema located at Wales. The owner, Lee, would let the driver of a car, which brought patrons of the cinema from outlying areas, go to any section of the cinema free of charge. Although the Morris Oxford was a six-seater, we squeezed in as many as twelve people, with some passengers sitting on the laps of others. Very often, one passenger sat on the hood of the car and another on in the open trunk. The passengers always included our cousin Ramadhin.

The police did not bother us for two reasons. The car was a private car, and there were no restrictions on the number of passengers, unlike the situation with hire cars, in which the passengers were limited to five. Another reason was that I was teaching at Wales Presbyterian School, located next to the police station and knew all the policemen at that station.

On one occasion, a policeman on a motor-cycle, based in the Vreedenhoop Police Station, stopped us when I was perched on the hood of the car, and warned me that I was risking my life. He said that he would not give me and the driver a ticket, if I promised not to do so again. I gave him my word, which I am not ashamed to admit that I did not keep, and he let us go.

After dropping most of the passengers home, we went to our own home, or to the home of one of our friends to savor a bottle or two of *El Dorado* rum. The alcohol always stimulated our appetites and we would want something to eat after a few drinks. Meat was preferable, along with some boiled rice, and we usually killed one of the chickens belonging to the owner of the house in which we were drinking..

Noor, one of the passengers, was a strapping youth whose only fault, as far as we were concerned, was that he ate beef. As Hindus, we considered the cow sacred, and ate no beef. However, his affable and helpful nature far outweighed this minor shortcoming, especially although most of us wanted to eat meat when we were drinking, many of us were reluctant to kill and prepare the chicken. Noor's father was a butcher and he was an expert in catching, killing, feathering, preparing and cooking the chickens. His mantra was: "I don't need any knife. Too much blood," as he prepared to wring the neck of a chicken. He was also a take-charge man who delegated responsibilities for who cooked the rice, and added the masala and garlic to the pot. Everybody appreciated his skills— the main reason why the group asked him the stick with us, when the other passengers were not invited. We enjoyed this routine for several weeks, in spite of the several admonishments from Ma.

"I knew this gon happen," she told Daddy. "Before you buy the car, dem boys gon go to Prag on Saturday, take a few drinks, and then come home. Now they take a whole clique to *The Plaza*, and then drink for most of the night. Next morning, they can't wake up, and they don't study."

One moonlit Saturday night, the usual group went to see *Deedar* at *The Plaza* and came back singing, *Bachapan Ka Dina Bhola Na Dena* out of tune all the way home. After dropping most of the passengers home, we stopped at Prag's Rum Shop at midnight. The shop was closed, but because it was owned by my father's sister, we were able to go to the back door and wake my aunt up. We bought two bottles of *El Dorado* rum and six Coca-Colas, because we did not want to buy only one bottle and run out of drinks. Ramadhin was so enchanted by *Deedar,* that he insisted on going to his place. Everybody felt at home there, because his father, who liked his sauce even more than we did, always joined us for our get-togethers. On one occasion he was very angry because we did wake him up.

As soon as we arrived at Ramadhin's house, we headed to the kitchen—a separate building from the house connected by a set of stairs. Ramadhin promptly went to the shelf with the glasses and brought six which he placed on the table. The extra glass was for his father, who would join us later. After opening a bottle of Coke using an opener hanging on a nail in the wall, he poured the first drink and passed the bottle around. When it was Noor's turn, he started to pour, but paused, with the neck of the bottle resting on the rim of the glass.

Noor said, "If we going to kill a fowl, we better do it now, before we get too drunk. Remember last week, Ramadhin? You get so drunk that you couldn't eat the chicken we cook at Dhanraj place. Leh we start cooking the chicken now, so that we all can eat. Then if you get drunk, you can sleep. At least you got something in yuh stomach."

Ramadhin stopped humming *Bachapan Ka Dina Bhola Na Deena*, and decided to usurp Noor's role. "You go and select any fowl, Noor. Deo, you know where the masala and everything is. Dhanraj can put on the rice to boil." After he assigned responsibilities, Ramadhin resumed the theme song.

Noor, who needed no prompting, left the kitchen, as Dhanraj poured kerosene on some kindling to get the fire going. I tried to remember in which cupboard I found the masala and garlic the last time we were at Ramadhin's, and opened the one on the right, which proved to be the correct one. Just as I started to mix the masala and garlic with water, Ramadhin's father walked in, his eyes heavy with sleep, but sleepy or not, he wasn't going to miss the opportunity to have a few drinks. Ramadhin stopped humming when his father entered the kitchen, and poured a drink for his dad, because his dad always liked him to pour the first drink for him. Then he resumed humming.

After a short while, he began to feel uneasy, but couldn't pinpoint the specific reason for his uneasiness. He stopped humming, wracked his brain in his attempt to identify the cause and suddenly remembered that his favorite rooster slept on the lowest branch of the nearest tree. He sprang out of his chair, upsetting his glass and spilling his drinks, bolted out of the kitchen and rushed to the orange tree.

Ramadhin felt relieved when he saw Noor standing under the tree, and rationalized that Noor had not selected any fowl yet. However, something fluttering on the ground caught his eye. At first, he refused to look closely, but he eventually willed himself to direct his eyes to the object and was able to determine that it was a chicken.

Perhaps it's another fowl, he told himself hopefully.

With halting steps, he picked up the chicken, whose fluttering was beginning to cease. He saw the red feathers and the red coxcomb, of which he was so proud. Reluctantly, the grieving Ramadhin was forced to accept that it was his rooster. He cradled it, put its head along his arm, and caressed its feathers.

"Not this one," he told Noor

"See if it living," Noor replied, consoling. "If it living, put it back on the branch."

Ramadhin glanced at the rooster. The fluttering had stopped, and he started to cry, as Noor gently took the rooster from his hand.

"Not that one! Not that one!" Ramadhin repeated between sobs.

In the kitchen, the fire was going and we all heard the interaction between Ramadhin and Noor. When we hustled outside, we saw Noor attempting to put his arm around Ramadhin's shoulder to console him, while holding the rooster in the other hand, and Ramadhin kept brushing it away. Then, Ramadhin suddenly broke away from the group and headed to the kitchen, poured half a tumbler of rum and drank it all in four gulps, while he sobbed intermittently.

That night, we had to make do with a little less rum, but we all had a bit more chicken, because while Ramadhin drank more than his share of rum, he refused eat anything. When we offered him some rice and just the gravy, without any meat, he shook his head and repeated his mantra, *Not that one.*

Nobody was surprised when Ramadhin swore off chicken for an entire year.

For weeks after this incident, there was a hiatus on the Saturday night trips to *The Plaza*, but eventually we were able to resume, after convincing Ramadhin to join us. However, we had to make a major concession. *No killing and eating chicken after the cinema.*

At home, Ramadhin's eating habits also changed. He ate his meals in the kitchen for a long time, instead of at the bottom house.

11 THE PUPIL TEACHER WHO MADE AN UPSIDE DOWN EIGHT

I was a shy fourteen-year-old when my brother, Andrew, and I passed the Pupil Teachers' Appointment Examination, which qualified us to be hired as pupil teachers. We had attended the Perpetua Kawall Canadian Mission School in the rural district of Canal Number 2 Polder. Our parents were devout Hindus. We were brought up as Hindus, but nearly all of the schools in Guyana were managed by Christian missionaries, and they hired only teachers who were baptized in their denominations.

Our parents were determined that their children would be successful educationally and told us, "If they want you to be baptized, then baptize, but just remember you will always be a Hindu. No White man gon sprinkle some water on you and make you a Christian."

Andrew was hired as a pupil teacher at Affiance Methodist School on the Essequibo Coast, after he was baptized by the Methodist minister, and I was hired at Wales Canadian Mission School, after being baptized in the Presbyterian Church. I rarely came out of Canal and it was an adventure for me to go to Wales, even though it was only nine miles away.

There was no university in Guyana at that time and only a handful of people who could afford the finances to study at the University of the West Indies or a university in England could earn a degree. No wonder that people who had degrees were well respected in the country.

As teachers, we used to say, "If a man has a BA Honors degree, you have to honor him." This held true, regardless of the area of study.

The structure of the education system in Guyana was quite different from the system in Canada and the United States, where there are boards of education in different areas, with the provincial or state Ministries of Education working with the various boards to coordinate the implementation of education policies. In Guyana, there was a central Ministry of Education, based in Georgetown, with branches in different parts of the country. The Ministry hired inspectors, who visited and evaluated schools in the entire country. Their inspections included the performance of the headmasters or headmistresses, and the teachers. It was therefore a traumatic experience for personnel.

On a fine, sunny Friday morning, Wales Canadian Mission School received a visit from Mr. Sylvester, a school inspector, who had recently returned to Guyana after earning a degree in geology. Why Mr. Sylvester did not seek and obtain employment in his area of expertise still remains a mystery to me, but when he darkened the entrance of the main door of our school, we were all nervous, although nobody was unduly worried.

The headmaster, Mr. S.I. Das, was an unassuming and kind man, but a stickler for observing the rules established by the Ministry. Our *Notes of Lessons* were up to date; our weekly education journals, specifying what we had taught for each week, were recorded, and our neat attendance registers were complete for the day, a / for students present, a *0* for students absent.

Mr. Sylvester was a huge man with a booming voice and his entire manner exuded bluster and confidence. He moved from classroom to classroom as a general would move from troop to troop on the parade square. Eventually, he reached my classroom, where I was teaching an arithmetic lesson in long division. I was quite proud of my prowess in arithmetic and proceeded to teach my lesson confidently, until a hand reached over my shoulder and I saw a thumb almost as large as the handle of a cricket bat, on the blackboard. I was quite sure that I had written 875 on the blackboard, but when I looked, I saw only 75. *What happened to the 8?* I asked myself.

"What's this?" Mr. Sylvester asked me in a voice loud enough for the entire class to hear.

I still don't know why I said, "Sorry," but I did, as I replaced the *8* on the blackboard. Mr. Sylvester smirked as he left to *inspect* another classroom.

After school, at the staff meeting mandated by Mr. Sylvester, the inspector commented on the areas in which the school did well, and the areas in which we needed to improve. "I like the fact that your attendance registers are neat and accurate," he told the staff. "And your *Notes of Lessons* and *Journals* are detailed. I like what Mr. Das is doing in this school."

Then he announced in his booming voice, "I saw a pupil teacher make an upside-down eight."

My entire body and mind were on high alert and my heart raced, because I was quite certain that his announcement was related to his thumb on my blackboard.

Mr. Sylvester looked at me sternly, saw my face mirroring my anxiety, and decided to remove all doubt from my mind and from the minds of the two other pupil teachers. I shrank in my seat as he pointed to me with his humongous index finger and pronounced, "Young man, I'm talking about you."

The entire staff was silent, no doubt ruminating on my grievous error, and I felt extreme gratitude to Mr. T.A.J. Singh, the deputy headmaster, a teetotaler and a frank speaker, when he came to my rescue. "He probably wrote it that way since Standard One, but we all recognize his eight."

Mr. Sylvester was stumped, and frowned as he moved on to other areas of the school. Imagine my relief when the meeting was over.

Afterwards, as I reflected on his comments about my upside-down eight, I wondered whether, on his return to the office of Ministry of Education in Georgetown, and in his report to the Chief Education Officer, did Mr. Sylvester tell him, "One of my biggest accomplishments was that I acquainted the staff that one of the pupil teachers made an upside-down eight?"

The following day, I consulted with the Standard One teacher, Mrs. Persaud, a kind and helpful lady, about the correct way to make an *8*, and practiced writing it for a while. In spite of my shyness, I had the utmost confidence in my academic ability and continued my teaching career with some success.

After I graduated from teachers' college, I joined the Guyana Defence Force as an officer, rose to the rank of captain, and was appointed as the A.D.C. to the President of Guyana. Just before schools closed for the summer holidays, the President hosted a function to recognize the role of the Ministry of Education in promoting the arts in the schools in Guyana and several education officials were invited.

It was a cool evening and many of the guests already had quite a few drinks under their belts as they mixed and mingled on the large green lawn of Guyana House, when the band struck the National Anthem and the President made his appearance, accompanied by yours truly. I moved freely among the guests, chatting and talking about the education of our greatest resource, our children.

Eventually, I joined a group of officials from the Ministry of Education, who were talking animatedly about the renaissance of art in our schools. One man stood out from the others because of his size and his voice, and I instantly recognized Mr. Sylvester, although the bald center of his head was ringed by lush grey hair, and he was slightly stooped.

Apparently, he had retained the position of school inspector and had still neglected to make practical use of his mining degree. He looked at me in my impressive dress uniform. Guyanese had recently freed themselves from the shackles of colonialism, under which all the important positions in Guyana, including the posts of the Governor-General and A.D.C., were held by people who were White. People in an independent Guyana were quite proud of the fact that these positions were then filled by Guyanese.

"Young man," Mr. Sylvester smiled as he addressed me. "You look very handsome. We are very proud that people like yourself can be in these positions."

All the rules of etiquette and good manners dictated that I should have simply said, "Thank you! You are very kind."

However, my pride in reaching the position that I did in the army, prompted by my huge ego, and the recollection of the humiliation I experienced at the hands of Mr. Sylvester when I was a young pupil teacher, made me neglect the above rules.

Even as I write this, I do not regret the fact that I turned to him, smiled confidently and told him, "Mr. Sylvester, you may or may not remember me. You visited Wales Canadian Mission School many years ago, and drew the attention of the entire staff on how a pupil teacher made an upside down *eight*. I was the pupil teacher who made the upside-down *eight*."

12 DO NOT SPEAK FOR TWO DAYS

My brother, Balo, twenty years old, was the sixth of the nine children my parents had. He lived with Ma and Daddy, along with the two youngest children, Chaman and Lorraine, in a sugar-estate housing project at Prospect Village, on the east bank of the Demerara River, about five miles south of Georgetown.

As a graduate from the University of Guyana, Balo was a well-paid teacher, who gave deeper meanings to the words, *kindness* and *unselfishness*. Because he was high earning and single, most members of the family, including yours truly, requested financial help from him, which he unhesitatingly granted. His soft voice and endearing manner genuinely came from a pure heart and unblemished mind.

Balo. tall, fair and slim, with brown eyes, had dark, black hair, which he kept shoulder length. He had our mother's nose, which curved slightly downward, and was the object of admiration of many young women as he rode his Suzuki motorcycle to and from the high school at Craig Village, about three miles away, where he taught English Language and Literature.

Try as he might, Balo could not get rid of a persistent cold and cough, which he had been battling for over two weeks. He stubbornly refused to see a doctor, in spite of numerous exhortations from Ma, Daddy and his younger siblings. Nobody complained, but Balo's high-pitched coughing frequently woke everybody in the house at nights.

Our vigorous fifty-seven-year-old father, was five feet, ten inches tall. He still had a full head of grey hair, which he kept in a crew cut. Although he had grown a stomach, his bicep muscles were still firm and his massive chest strained against his tight shirt. The years he had spent working in our farm in Canal No. 2 Polder, before we moved to Prospect, had toughened his body, although had given up farming about five years earlier and had bought a clothing business at Stabroek Market in Georgetown.

Daddy, who ruled the house with an iron hand, stuttered whenever he was angry or upset. Everybody, including our mother, a frail soft-spoken woman, who made many sacrifices to maintain a peaceful household, knew to keep quiet whenever he started to stutter.

On the Saturday morning of the third week of Balo's cold and cough, Daddy was sitting at the kitchen table, eating his breakfast of roti and *bhaigan choka*—fried boulangers mixed with a variety of spices—when Balo started emitting an ear-piercing cough in his bedroom. The walls of our house, like the walls of most houses in Guyana at that time, did not reach up to the ceiling. A space of about three feet between the top of the wall and the ceiling facilitated free air flow in the hot tropical country. Unfortunately, this type of construction also allowed sounds to carry across the house. When Balo continued coughing for a long time, everybody stopped and listened with a great deal of concern.

Daddy put down his cup of coffee and told Ma, "That boy got a cough and cold for over two weeks now, and he don't want to see a doctor. He cough so much last night that I couldn't sleep. He don't care about himself at all. I gon carry him to Dr. Ramroop today."

"I tell him over and over to go and see a doctor and get some medicine for the cough," Ma replied. "I glad you gon take him to the doctor. I gon go and wake him up."

Ma left the kitchen and knocked at Balo's door. "Wake up Balo, brush your teeth, and eat something. Then put on yuh good clothes. Your dad gon take you to a doctor for your cough."

"I gon feel better, once I get some more rest," Balo responded, between coughs. He felt extremely tired, and would have liked to remain in bed for an hour or two more.

Daddy heard Balo response, left his breakfast, and joined Ma at the door. "Yooou reeest laaang eeenough. And tttthe rrrum yyou drrrink mmmek things wworst."

Once he heard the stuttering, Balo reluctantly got out of bed and came out of his bedroom without further objections. He carefully

71

avoiding looking anybody in the eye, or speaking to anybody, especially Daddy, went sullenly to the kitchen, and grabbed his toothbrush. He filled a cup with water and went to the porch to brush his teeth.

When he entered the kitchen reluctantly, visibly upset at being taken to see a doctor against his will, Ma had already dished out a plate of roti and *baigan choka* before him. She endeavored to placate him as she placed a cup of coffee before him.

"You Daddy worried about you," she told him in a soothing voice. "Remember last month Sugrim had a cold and cough, and he so stubborn that he didn't go to see the doctor, although his mummy and daddy tell him over and over to go and see a doctor. And he dead of pneumonia? Go to the doctor and get some medicine for your cold. I don't know if you have pneumonia already, and I don't want anything to happen to you. Besides, you talk in front of all the school children. I don't want them to scorn you because you got a cough."

None of my siblings would give a harsh response to Ma, and Balo, perhaps the most sensitive of all of the children, was no exception. He grunted something which sounded like an assent and proceeded to eat his breakfast and drink his coffee.

Ma's talk apparently also calmed Daddy, who stopped his stuttering and went in his room to change. After he finished breakfast, Balo also changed his clothes and was ready to use his motorcycle to ride to Georgetown, with Daddy as a pillion rider.

'You got a bad cough and cold, and you want to ride yuh motorcycle to Georgetown?" Daddy told him. "Leh we take a hire car, so you can rest."

Balo was compliant and he and Daddy flagged a hire car on the East Bank Road, which took them to the hire car park, near Stabroek Market. From there, it was a fifteen-minute walk to Dr. Ramroop's office in Brickdam.

Dr. Ramroop had his consulting practice under his house and he lived on the upper floor. Almost all of the folding chairs he had set out in the waiting room for patients were filled and Daddy and Balo took two of the three vacant chairs, after checking in with the receptionist.

As they prepared for the long wait, Daddy turned to Balo. "Since we here already, and we got to wait so long, I gon ask Dr. Ramroop about my nose. I gon find out from him why I can't smell. I see three doctors already, and all of them take my money, but none of them tell me why I can't smell."

Balo stopped coughing. "It must be a blockage in your nose."

"It can't be a blockage. Remember Dr. Singh charge me one hundred dollars to do an operation to clear the nose, but I still can't smell. I go back to him, and he give me three kind of nose drop, and still I can't smell. Dr. Ramroop is a good doctor, and I gon ask him why I can't smell."

Daddy and Balo waited three hours to see Dr. Ramroop and Balo was a captive audience for Daddy's recounting the history of his smelling woes. At times, Balo didn't really have to cough, but he went into fits of coughing just so that he could get a break from hearing about Daddy's lack of smell and the different remedies he had tried. When the receptionist finally called Balo's name, he was extremely relieved.

As soon as Balo and Daddy returned from the doctor and Daddy opened the door and entered the house, Ma asked anxiously, "What the doctor say? He gave Balo any medicine? Weh Balo?"

Daddy put his hands to his lips, pointed to himself, and shook his head from side to side.

Ma was flabbergasted. "Something happened with Balo? Tell me!" Meanwhile, Chaman and Lorraine were mesmerized by Daddy's non-verbal gestures—wondering whether something had happened to Balo, and that Daddy was feeling too emotional to speak.

Ma started to tremble and sat on the sofas, while Daddy kept pointing to his lips and shaking his head. Chaman and Lorraine sat beside Ma to comfort her. Imagine their relief when Balo walked through the door a few minutes later. He had stopped to make some minor adjustments to his motorbike which was parked under the house, before coming upstairs.

Ma, greatly relieved, got up as soon as Balo entered the house, put her hand on his arm and asked him, "Balo what happen? You okay?"

"Yes Ma! The doctor gave me some medicine and some antibiotic tablets. He say I gon be okay. He say that I must rest and take the tablet until it finish. But I can't drink until the tablet finish."

"Okay! You must not drink while you taking the tablets. Don't let yuh friends force you to tek even one drink. You know how rum go. Once you tek one, yuh can't stop. Why you daddy don't speak?"

"Oh! The doctor told him not to speak for two days. Dr. Ramroop tell him that he might be able to smell again and may even be able to speak better, but that he must not talk for two days."

For the reader to comprehend why Daddy followed the doctor's instructions to the letter, he must understand the social situation in Guyana, and the role doctors played in the Guyanese society at that time. With only a few qualified doctors in the country, those who wanted to consult a doctor had to travel to the major cities and wait a long time. Some might not be able to see the doctor and would have to return the following day. It was no wonder that the few doctors in the country were regarded as minor Gods, and their instructions were followed implicitly.

When Daddy left to visit the latrine, Balo recounted what transpired in the doctor's office. As soon as he and Daddy went in Dr. Ramroop's office, Daddy told the doctor about his nose—about how he couldn't smell. Then he complained about Dr. Singh and the other doctors he saw—how they took his money and didn't do anything to make him smell again.

The doctor looked at the file before him and asked Daddy, "The file says that Balo Rampersaud is the patient. Are you Balo Rampersaud?"

"No," Daddy replied, "Balo Rampersaud is my son. He has a bad cough, but since I here, I say that I gon ask you why I can't smell."

Dr. Ramroop was tired and impatient after seeing so many patients, and he thought about the number of patients waiting outside. He put down his pen, faced Daddy, and told him, "From now on, I don't want you to talk for two days." Daddy started to ask for an explanation, but Dr. Ramroop put his right palm outwards to face Daddy. "Heh eh! Not a word for two days."

Then he put his index finger on his lips and repeated, "Two days! Okay? You may be able to smell after you do not talk for two days."

After giving Daddy the above instructions, the doctor turned to Balo. "Why did you come to see me?"

Balo told the doctor about his cough and Dr. Ramroop prescribed some cough medicine and antibiotic tablets. "Take these until they are all finished, and the cold and cough should go away. Do not drink any alcohol while you're taking the antibiotic tablets. If your cough doesn't go away, come back and see me, and I will give you something stronger."

"Thank you doctor. I can't even take a small drink when I'm taking the tablets?" Balo asked hopefully.

"Not even a small drink," Dr. Ramroop emphasized.

Daddy decided to make one last try. "Doctor …"

Dr. Ramroop looked at him, put his finger to his lips, and repeated, "Two days! Remember!" Then before Daddy could remonstrate, he opened the door to his office, and shouted to his receptionist, "NEXT!"

And that is why Daddy communicated with non-verbal gestures for two whole days.

13 DRINKING CERVEZAS AT THE PEGASUS OR A TALE OF TWO LANGUAGES

"*H*ow about some beers at the Pegasus?" Rao, scion of a wealthy window manufacturing family, told me and my brothers, Abel, and Balram, as he patted his well-padded wallet with his right hand.

A six-footer, who exuded confidence with his booming voice, long beard, and self-assured bearing, Rao was drinking rum and coke with us at my newly built home in Meadowbrook Gardens, an upscale neighborhood, which was a government project. Housing lots were sold at well below the market price, to public officials and I was able to secure one of these lots because I was ADC to the President.

I was also able to secure a large enough loan from *The New Building Society* to build a rather nice house. The cost of the house lot, and instalments on the loan had left me with just a trickle of cash flow.

I had known Rao when he installed the windows in my home, and he had attached himself to me because his family already had wealth, and they made a great deal of effort to establish and maintain contact with people in well-placed positions.

Abel my elder brother was the headmaster of Bonasika Primary School, and his wife was teaching in the same school. A heavy drinker, Abel visited our parents at Prospect, on the East Bank of the Demerara River, every weekend and invariably got soused whenever he visited.

On this Saturday afternoon, Rao and I were having the first drink from a bottle of El Dorado rum, when I was pleasantly surprised to see Balram riding towards my home on his Suzuki motorcycle, with Abel as the pillion rider.

Balram, twenty-three years old, had graduated from the

University of Guyana, which its detractors called *Jagan Night School*, two years earlier with a B.A. in English Literature. He was unmarried, living with our parents, and we were all aware that many mothers of single daughters had designs on him. He was a fair, handsome guy, who was always clean-shaven, with his long, black hair neatly combed, and his shoes always polished to a shine.

It was a puzzle to all his friends how Balram managed to keep his shoes so clean, even when the roads were muddy. If the truth be told, he was once told by a girl with whom he was deeply infatuated, that she could always tell the quality of a guy by looking at his hair and his shoes. From that day on, Balram ensured that he had an adequate supply of brillantine hair gel, and polished his shoes every day. He even kept a cloth in his back pocket to wipe them ever so often.

We jumped at Rao's offer. Pegasus, located on Seawall Road, was next to the Atlantic Ocean, and consequently had nothing between it and the refreshing Northeast Trade Winds. It was the newest, most upscale hotel in Georgetown, and indeed in Guyana. I might add, it was also the most expensive one. Only members of the upper tier of the society in Guyana, tourists, and wealthy merchants like Rao, could afford to stay at this exclusive hotel, or eat or drink at the restaurant and bar on its main floor.

Rao scowled when Abel and Balram refused his offer to ride in his brand-new, blue Ford pick-up truck, and elected to join me in my old mini-cooper. He was looking forward to showing off his powerful vehicle.

I lost sight of the Ford almost as soon as we left Meadowbrook Gardens, as Rao weaved through traffic and even drove through a red light. The powerful engine of the Ford allowed him to leave us comfortably behind, as my old mini-cooper sputtered along, and strained to gain momentum after we stopped at traffic lights.

When I pulled into the parking lot of the tall and majestic Pegasus, Rao had already parked, and was standing by the entrance of the hotel. I was grateful that he invited us for beers at a very prestigious hotel.

Rao wore a pair of grey serge trousers and a Hawaiian shirt adorned with palm trees on the beach of an extremely blue ocean. I thought that his outfit was ideal for the Pegasus and couldn't help looking down at my old, grey tennis shirt. Then I glanced at Abel and Balram, who were not dressed any better, and wondered whether our decision to go to the Pegasus on that particular day was a good one.

As we started to walk towards the hotel, I thought that it was an excellent opportunity to practice Spanish with Balram, who had completed the required Spanish courses at the University of Guyana. I had recently enrolled at that university and constantly questioned the university's requirements that students had to take either Spanish or French as a required course. I had enrolled in the Spanish course, because I was told that it was easier to learn Spanish than French. Having had no previous exposure to Spanish, I was having problems learning this language, and I knew I was not ready for the end-of-year examinations to be held in a few months.

I greeted Rao. "Hola amigo," but after he gave me a puzzled look, I ignored him and turned to Balram.

"Como estas?" I asked, as we made our way to the lounge.

Balram looked at his shoes before replying, "Muy bien, gracias."

We entered the lounge, selected a table which allowed us to have a clear view of the Atlantic Ocean, and I continued practicing Spanish with Balram, ignoring Abel and Rao, who probably felt totally sidelined.

After a few minutes, the waiter, dressed in a white jacket and black trousers, and sporting a black bow tie, approached our table. I was anxious to practice my Spanish and forgot that it was Rao, with the padded wallet, who had invited us, and therefore it was his right to order.

"Cuatro cervezas por favor," I ordered, in what I hoped was good Spanish.

The waiter apparently knew, or at least, understood Spanish, and left immediately to fetch us the beers, as Balram and I continued conversing in Spanish. Rao abruptly left without saying a word to anyone, but Balram and I, immersed in our Spanish conversation, did not even realize that the person whose wallet was bulging, and who invited us. was no longer present. We were also ignoring Abel, who did not understand Spanish..

Abel, tall and lean, sat at the table looking intensely at me and Balram. It was the first time he had been at the Pegasus and was understandably frustrated and upset that his brothers insisted in speaking a language he did not understand. When the waiter eventually arrived and put four beers on the table, Abel reached for a beer and started sipping it without saying a word.

"Muy bien cerveza," I observed to Balram as I sipped the cold beer.

"Si," Balram responded. "Mas major que el ron," indicating that the beer was better than rum.

Abel was silent as he looked sullenly around the lounge, where several well-to-do people were enjoying their assorted drinks. Even as Balram and I were busy practicing our Spanish, I noticed Abel's hand shaking slightly as he raised his beer to his mouth. I am ashamed to say that we continued in this manner until we finished our beers.

We were in the process of sharing the fourth beer intended for Rao, when the waiter approached and asked me, because I was the person who ordered the first round, "Would you like another round, sir?"

I would have liked another beer, but remembered that I had no money, and the person whose pockets were always bulging, was no longer with us.

"Nada," I told the waiter.

"That will be fifteen dollars, sir," the waiter said.

"Quince dollars" I told Balram. "Tiene usted dinero?" (Do you have money?)

"No tengo dinero," Balram replied, and we both looked at Abel, earnestly hoping that he had at least fifteen dollars.

After an uncomfortable silence, Abel looked at me squarely and replied, "You ordered them in Spanish. Pay for them in English," as he leaned back in his chair smiling.

I immediately forgot to speak in Spanish. "I don't have any money," I told him.

"You ordered them in Spanish. Pay for them in English," Abel repeated, with what appeared to be a smirk.

The waiter immediately sensed that there was going to be a problem. He went behind the counter, picked up a phone, dialed a number, and then hung up. In a few minutes, a burly guy with long hair, and wearing a tight blue T-shirt and a beard appeared and initiated a conversation with the waiter. When he glanced in our direction, I knew that we were the subject of the discussion.

Then I remembered my cheque book.

"That's security," I told Balram and Abel, as I reached into my pocket, pulled out my cheque book, and motioned to the waiter. "I just remembered that I have my cheque book. I can write you a cheque." After he hesitated, I emphasized, "IN ENGLISH," as I flashed my cheque book.

"You should have told us that before you ordered. We can do nothing when you walk out of here, and your cheque bounces."

The waiter raised his voice and looked at the security guy. I noticed that he had dropped the appellation, "Sir." The other patrons in the lounge were staring at us and I hoped that no one recognized me.

Abel observed everything with a smile, and obviously enjoyed seeing me sweat. At that time, there were no visa cards and no ATM machines, so it appeared as we were doomed to be embarrassed.

"Well, I have only my cheque book and no money, so what do you want me to do?" I asked the waiter.

By this time, the security guard had approached our table, and addressed me directly. "We're going to call the police," he said. "It is fraud if you order drinks, knowing that you have no money to pay for them."

Then he turned and started to walk towards the phone behind the counter, when Abel interrupted.

"How much did you say the bill was?"

"Fifteen dollars," the waiter replied glumly, as the security guy hesitated.

I breathed a loud sigh of relief as Abel pushed his hand in his pocket, pulled out a roll of bills, peeled out three five-dollar bills and handed them to the waiter, who accepted it with a scowl and returned to his place behind the bar.

You had the money all this time, and you made us sweat, I thought, as I looked at my elder brother with a mixture of gratitude and frustration.

We avoided looking at the other customers as we got up, slunk out of the lounge and quickly left the hotel. We did not look back as we hastened towards my mini-cooper to distance ourselves from the source of our discomfort.

As I turned the key in the ignition and the engine sputtered and then started, Abel turned to me smugly and asked, "Are we going back to your place to drink some more rum. Or do you have any dinero to buy more cervezas?"

"Beer will always be beer with me from now on. Never again will *beer* be *cervezas*," I retorted as the mini cooper groaned its way towards Meadowbrook.

14 MANGROO AND DISPENSER LIVERPOOL

Sixty-two-year-old Mangroo lived about half a mile from the school, the dispensary, and the community center, which was considered the hub of the country district of Canal No. 2 Polder.

Mangroo was quite short, but was heavily built and was almost as tall as he was wide. His friends initially called him "Square," but the name didn't take, because Mangroo refused to answer to it. In addition to his square build, the most distinguishing feature of Mangroo, and the feature of which he was most proud, was his very large moustache, which was so huge that it protruded from the sides of his face.

Mangroo owned a house and about a mile of land behind it. Most of his land, like the other properties in Canal, was covered with coffee trees and provision farms. While the income from the coffee reaped from these trees and the produce from the provision farms did not make for a luxurious lifestyle, it was enough for Mangroo and son Dalo, "to keep body and soul together," especially since most of their meals consisted of provisions or vegetables reaped from their farm.

He and Dalo had gone to consult a lawyer in Georgetown in order to put Dalo as the joint owner of the property, and Mangroo consoled himself that his only son would inherit his house and land

Dalo, a handsome guy of about twenty-five, never attended school, because Mangroo had refused to let him learn *backra language,*[17] and the two were content to communicate in *Creole*, a mixture of languages with its own complex grammar. In fact, father and son considered themselves quite happy and self-sufficient, in the little farming community

Some years earlier, Mangroo had become incensed at the English

---

[17] Language of the White man

when a White overseer kicked him from his horse. The overseer had asked Mangroo to carry him across a drainage/transportation canal because he wanted to inspect the sugar cane plants on the other side, but he didn't want to get his boots and trousers wet.

"I come here to cut cane, not to let any White man ride me like the horse yuh riding now," Mangroo had replied to the overseer, who had lashed out with his leg in response. The leg contacted Mangroo's face, but left him with more emotional than physical pain.

Another muscular cane-cutter, Abdul, to the chagrin of Mangroo, had offered to take the overseer across the canal. After the overseer left, Mangroo pointed his cutlass at Abdul, and taunted, "Next time, the overseer gon want ride yuh ass."

Mangroo, a very headstrong and opinionated individual, realized that he could do nothing in retaliation against the overseer and vowed that he would never again work on the sugar estate. He concentrated on his coffee and provision farm and isolated himself, and unfortunately his family, from the world outside of Canal as much as possible.

**

Dalo's mother, Sudini, had passed away five years earlier. She had a cold, and Mangroo had insisted that she take *bush medicine,*[18] prescribed by Edna, who lived five lots away, and was the acknowledged expert in this area. Edna had successfully treated the family for minor illnesses in the past, and Mangroo had complete confidence in her, but unfortunately her cure was not successful in that particular case. Sudini's cold had developed into pneumonia and she tragically passed away in her sleep.

**

One morning, as they were eating breakfast before going to weed the coffee farm, Dalo noticed that his father's cough was getting worse, and that the mucus coming out of his nose was yellow. In addition, his voice was so hoarse that Dalo could hardly understand

---

[18] Herbal remedies

what his father was saying.

"Daddy, yuh got that cold for a long time now, and it getting worse. You got to tek some medicine fuh it."

"Ah gon drink some fever grass tea when I come home dis afternoon," Mangroo replied as he drained his cup of coffee.

"I don't want you to weed *coffee walk*[19] with a cold. Stay home today, and go to Dispenser Liverpool. He good, and he cure many people."

Mangroo and Balo had given up Edna and her bush cures after the death of Balo's mother, but were never ill enough to go to Dispenser Liverpool, the village dispenser.

The building which housed the dispensary was divided into two sections. The section nearest the bridge leading to the school and the dispensary was designated as the consulting and treatment room, with a waiting area containing a number of benches with no back rests. The second section contained the living quarters for Dispenser Liverpool and his family.

"I gon work fuh half-day, and then come home and rest," Mangroo conceded.

"Yuh remember wha' happen to Ma? Yuh want the same thing to happen to you? I gon get married in three month, and I want you to stand father for me at the wedding. You go and see Dispenser Liverpool. I can come wid you if you want."

"The coffee walk need weeding. Why you want to come wid me? You sick too?"

Dalo recognized that, with no other income than the coffee and provision farms, it was important that they kept on top of things. "All right!" he told his father. "You go and see Dispenser Liverpool. I think dat he open the dispensary at half past eight, but go early because a lot of people gon want to see him. Dis flu season bad. I gon go and weed the coffee walk. Make sure that you tek the medicine he give you right away."

---

[19] Coffee farm

Dalo left to go to the coffee farm at about 7:30, but before leaving, he repeated his exhortations to his father, "Mek sure that you go and see Dispenser Liverpool. And mek sure that you take the medicine he give you."

After Balo left, Mangroo remembered that the fever grass plants were just fifty yards behind the latrine, and was tempted to cut some, make some fever grass tea, and rest after drinking the tea, but he remembered his promise to his son. He took a quick shower at the standpipe, using a bucket and a calabash, changed into his *going out* clothes and headed to the dispensary, fifteen minutes' walk away.

When he arrived at the dispensary at about 8:15, it was not yet open and there were four women sitting close together in the waiting room. He looked at the women, thought that it was not fitting that he should sit with them, and opted to sit at the end of one bench as far from the women as possible.

After about ten minutes, the door separating the living quarters from the dispensary opened, and Dispenser Liverpool nodded to the people in the waiting room. "Good Morning."

Previously, Mangroo had seen Dispenser Liverpool riding his bicycle to visit a few villagers who were too ill to go to the dispensary, but it was the first time he was seeing the dispenser up close. Dispenser Liverpool was a tall, slim man, with sparse hair on his head. He was always immaculately dressed, with his shoes polished to a shine. The dispenser always wore a tie, regardless of how warm it was. He exhibited a warm, but formal and business-like manner to his patients, no doubt developed after his experience with many of the villagers' inquisitiveness and tendency to gossip. Many patients had previously attempted to probe into the illnesses of other villagers and Dispenser Liverpool always responded with a firm question of his own.

"Are you here to talk about the illnesses of other people, or are you here because you are ill?"

When word got around the village about his no-nonsense approach, nobody attempted to get insights into the illnesses of their friends or enemies from the dispenser, who refused to listen to the idle gossip many patients offered.

Five minutes after he opened the door to his dispensary, the dispenser poked his head out of the door and asked, "Who's first?"

A middle-aged woman got up with difficulty and walked into the dispensary holding her back with both hands.

She got back pain, Mangroo said to himself. While Dispenser Liverpool was treating the patient, Mangroo looked at the other patients and thought, *I wonder what wrong wid dem? Sumintra look like she got a cold, but the rest of dem don't look like they got flu.*

He remembered the rumors about five months earlier, when Mohamed told a friend that he had visited a prostitute in Georgetown and had contracted gonorrhea. By the following morning, most people in the village knew that Mohamed had *bad sick* and they wondered how many other people had it. Most villagers did not know much about the spread of the disease and were afraid of contracting it themselves. To protect themselves, his friends ensured that they did not pee in the same place that Mohamed peed on, did not drink from the same glass as he did, and did not go swimming in the conservancy canal with him.

I don't think that any of dem gat bad sick, Mangroo said to himself, as he looked at the women laughing and talking among themselves.

Mangroo was interrupted from his thoughts by Dispenser Liverpool opening the door, and asking, "Who's next?"

The next patient was Baboutie, who lived about a mile west of the school, and as she walked towards the dispenser, Mangroo noticed that she walked with a limp. Oddly enough, this relaxed him. *Oh! Something wrong with she foot. Nothing serious wrong wid she,* he thought.

By the time it was Mangroo's turn to see the dispenser, the waiting room was full and Mangroo couldn't help observing, *I didn't know Canal got so many sick people.* As he looked at the people he knew, he allowed his curiosity to get the better of him and he started to think of the various illnesses each of them might have, but his thoughts were interrupted by Dispenser Liverpool saying, "Who's next?"

As soon as he went into the treatment room, and before Dispenser Liverpool closed the door, Mangroo told him, "Doc, I got this cold a long, long time, and it wouldn't go away. Me son, Balo, frighten that I gon dead just like me wife."

Dispenser Liverpool knew everybody in village and knew about Sudini's death. "You should have brought her to see me. Bush medicine may work in some cases, but for pneumonia, she needed strong anti-biotics. You say that your nose is blocked up?"

"Yes Doc! Me nose stuff up, and the snot coming out very yellow and thick like condense milk. Also, me voice hoarse like crapaud. And me coughing like wan dog."

"Okay! I'll give you some strong medicine," Dispenser Liverpool told him, as he was pouring some liquid from a large bottle into a smaller one. Then he wrote, *Take one teaspoon three times a day* on a label, pasted the label on the bottle and passed the bottle to Mangroo.

"Mangroo, make sure that you finish all the medicine. If you don't feel better, come back, and I'll give you some antibiotic tablets."

Mangroo took the bottle from Dispenser Liverpool and clasped it to his breast as if he was given a treasure. "Thank you very much, Doc! I gon come back when I finish dis."

But Dispenser Liverpool was too busy calling the next patient to notice Mangroo's ecstasy. As Vardhan, an old man with a sore on his left ankle that wouldn't go away, and who was required to see the dispenser three times a week so that the sore could be cleaned and dressed, walked into the treatment room, Mangroo walked towards the bridge spanning the canal, known to everybody as *School Bridge*. This bridge was the best built bridge spanning the canal in the entire village and was wide enough so that a motorcyclist or a cyclist could ride across, but not wide enough to accommodate a car.

**

When Dispenser Liverpool was finished with Vadhan, he poked his head out the door, and asked, "Who's next?"

Then his eyes focused on Mangroo, who was standing and leaning against the railing of the verandah. "Mangroo, what are you doing here? I just saw you."

"You tell me to come back when the medicine finish, Doc. I finish it."

"You mean …" Then the truth dawned on Dispenser Liverpool. Mangroo could not read the instructions he had written on the label, and had taken all the medicine as soon as he had left the dispensary. "You got the empty bottle?" he asked Mangroo in a voice trembling with anxiety.

Mangroo proudly showed the empty bottle to the dispenser, who took it from him. He expected to be congratulated and was surprised when Dispenser looked at the road on which Budya's hire car was fortuitously approaching.

"BUDYA!" Dispenser Liverpool screamed. The urgency of the dispenser's voice caused Budya to stop his car suddenly, and the dispenser grabbed Mangroo by his arm and practically dragged him to Budya's car. "Take Mangroo to the hospital right away, and tell them that he drank all the medicine in this bottle at the same time. They will know what to do."

Dispenser Liverpool put the empty bottle in Budya's hand.

The people in Canal, with all their petty quarrels, their rum drinking, and their gossiping, were deeply loyal to each other, and Budya promptly opened the passenger side of the rear door, because the front seats were already taken. After Dispenser Liverpool pushed Mangroo in the car, Budya took off with a speed and did not stop for any other passengers who flagged him. It took him thirty-five minutes to pull into Vreedenhoop Police Station, a trip which would normally take nearly an hour, where he rushed to the police constable on duty.

"Mangroo drink all this cold medicine at the same time, and Dispenser Liverpool say that I got to take him to the hospital, or else he gon die. The next boat not until 12:00, and I asking that you get the police launch to take him to the hospital."

The police constable hesitated. "The police launch is only for police business," he told Budya hesitatingly.

"Mangroo almost dead now. Lemme talk to Sergeant Wilson. I know him."

Sergeant Wilson and Budya had shared many bottles of rum, bought by Budya, to ensure that he would not be harassed by the traffic police on motor-cycles, and be charged for *overloading*—having more passengers in the car that the law allowed. The police constable called Sergeant Wilson, who lived in the same compound, but in a separate house with his family. As soon as he heard Budya's name, Sergeant Wilson hurried over, anticipating a bottle of rum, but he was disappointed when Budya told him the same story he had told the police constable.

Sergeant Wilson picked up the hand radio. "Get the police launch ready for an emergency," he ordered. "A man overdosed on a medicine, and is in bad shape. He has to go to the Public Hospital right away."

Then he turned to Budya, "You go to the stelling. The launch will take you to Georgetown, and an ambulance will be waiting."

Accustomed to giving orders, Sergeant Wilson faced the police constable and instructed, "Call Georgetown and tell them to have an ambulance standing by. We have a case of serious overdose."

Then he asked Budya, "You have the bottle? Who gon go with this man to the hospital?"

Basil, who had accompanied Budya into the police station, promptly volunteered. "I gon go with him. I going to Georgetown only to buy a shovel, and that can wait."

"Give this man the bottle, so that the doctor can know what medicine he overdosed on," he told Budya. "And hurry to the stelling. The launch is ready."

As Budya turned to leave the station, Sergeant Wilson put his hand on Budya's shoulder. "We gon take a drink later?"

"Yes Sarge! I gon come early when I make the last trip for the five-thirty boat. We gon tek a few."

Sergeant Wilson smiled widely. "You better hurry. The launch is waiting."

Mangroo was taken to the hospital where they pumped the

medicine from his stomach and kept him in the hospital for a day. When Balo went to bring his father home, they were lucky to get Budya's car.

"Mangroo okay now?" Budya asked Balo.

"Yes Uncle! They pump he stomach."

"I glad," Budya responded. Then he remembered his own role in Mangroo's episode. "I also glad that I was passing by and was able to help. People in Canal travel with me fuh so long, I glad that I can help when I can."

Then the passengers talked about their coffee crops, and how they suspected that Coffee Baba was stealing some coffee beans from everybody who took their coffee to his factory to separate the beans from the pulp, before they moved to discussing other topics.

When they reached Canal and they passed the Dispensary, Budya, who had the reputation of teasing everybody if he was given the slightest reason, and had already sneaked in a few drinks even though it was only about 1:00 o'clock, told Mangroo, "The dispensary still open, Mangroo. You want to try another bottle?"

"It too late fuh me to learn to read. Next time, I gon ask Dispenser Liverpool to read the label fuh me," Mangroo told everybody in the car.

Then he asked Budya. "You gon tek a drink wid me? Rum bottle don't have label to tell you how much to drink."

15 DWARKA AND THE FLIGHT TO DOMINICA

My nineteen-year-old brother, Dwarka, was living with my parents at Prospect Village, a sugar estate housing scheme located on the East Bank of the Demerara River about six miles from Georgetown, the capital of Guyana. Dwarka, a teacher in Covent Garden Secondary School, was committed to making the world a better place. Always an extrovert and an excellent public speaker, Dwarka, tall and lean, with long hair and beard, was very active politically, and was also quite involved in the church.

When the formation of a Caribbean Community and Common Market (CARICOM) was being discussed, Dwarka wholeheartedly supported the initiative. He was well aware that, along with the many small island nations in the Caribbean, Guyana, with its population of 729 000, could not compete in the global economy on its own. The solution lay in the formation of CARICOM, basically a free trade agreement between the participating Caribbean nations.

There would be little or no tariffs on imports and exports, and no price controls, making the members of CARICOM a large economic community. Although Guyana was not geographically a part of the Caribbean, it was regarded as part of the English-speaking Caribbean economically and politically because it is the only English-speaking country in South America. With the newly independent nations exerting themselves to break the shackles of colonialism, CARICOM seemed like a very progressive initiative.

In the summer of 1970, his contacts in the government and church had ensured that Dwarka received an invitation to a conference to be held in the island of Dominica, to discuss the formation of CARICOM. He duly prepared for his first trip to a country outside of Guyana. As expected, there was a great deal of fuss about his leaving.

"Ma, I gon spend only one week, and them I gon come back," he reassured our mother, who was always stressed whenever any of her children ventured into unfamiliar territory, and was busy ironing his clothes and packing his suitcase. She was even going to put some fried fish and bread in his suitcase to ensure that he had "something to put in his stomach," when he interrupted her.

"Ma, I am not going to the bush. The government sending me to a conference, and they gon pay for the hotel and food. You don't have to pack any food for me," he assured her, causing her to reluctantly remove the fried fish and bread.

Ma, Daddy and Dwarka woke up at 5:00 a.m. on the day of Dwarka's departure because his flight was at 11:00 a.m., and Dwarka was supposed to be at the airport, about forty-five minutes away, at 8:00 a.m. However, Daddy always allowed himself some extra time, and insisted that they leave at 7:00.

"You never know what may happen," he emphasized. "There can be an accident which will delay us. Or you can have a flat, and it will take time to put on the spare tire. Even if we reach there early, it will be better than being late."

In situations like these, Daddy always concluded with, "The early bird catches the worm."

The trip to the airport was uneventful and the party was indeed early, causing Dwarka to take the opportunity to tease Daddy. "Daddy, we came early, but I don't see any worms to catch."

"If we come late, you na gon[20] even catch the plane," Daddy retorted.

After Dwarka checked in with Caribbean Airlines, they paid fifty cents each to go the VIP lounge, an enclosed area from which you can see the passengers board the plane, and witness the plane take off.

As soon as they entered the lounge, Daddy headed straight to the bar and Ma and Dwarka chose to sit at one of the tables.

Daddy was not accustomed to buying one drink, because the rum shops in Guyana usually sold alcoholic drinks by the bottle, the

---

[20] not going to

smallest bottle being a *quarter*. Most people would buy a quarter when they were alone, or with one friend, and they wanted one or two drinks.

When the bartender approached Daddy, my father promptly told him, "Is me alone. Give me a quarter bottle of rum."

The bartender obviously heard that request before, and patiently explained, "We don't sell rum by the bottle here like the rum shops. We sell only individual drinks. I can give you a double if you like."

"Bring the bottle and I gon pour fuh myself," Daddy requested.

"Sorry sir, I can't do that. You want a double or a single?"

By then, Daddy was feeling very thirsty and impatient and told the bartender, "Okay! Give me a double."

Daddy was fascinated as the bartender picked up a bottle of rum, with a contraption that regulated the flow of the drinks. He poured one drink, before putting the bottle upright and then poured another drink. Then the bartender asked, "Do you want Coke or Pepsi to mix it with?"

Daddy, who was accustomed to mixing his own drinks, hesitated before answering, "Coke, but not too much." He wanted to ask the bartender to allow him to mix his own chasers, but then he remembered what happened when he asked to pour his own drinks, and refrained from saying anything, although he liked to mix his drinks so that he could taste the rum.

He glanced at Ma and Dwarka as he took the first sip, and saw that Ma was talking earnestly to Dwarka, her entire facial expression displaying concern and anxiety. He remembered the newspaper column, four months previously in the *Daily Graphic* describing an airline crash in which 114 people died, but tried not to dwell on the incident. Daddy regretted sharing that specific article with Ma, because he knew that she would be also thinking about Dwarka flying and the airline crash.

He felt quite uncomfortable, because he was not accustomed to sit at a bar like the one he was sitting at, and the double he had ordered finished quite quickly. He missed having a bottle beside him so that he could pour another drink when he needed to, but he managed to catch the bartender's eyes.

"Another double, sir?" the bartender asked.

Daddy was accustomed to calling other people, especially White people, "Sir," but was not accustomed to be addressed by this title. He had no doubt that the bartender was speaking to him, because there was direct eye contact.

"Yes," he replied. Daddy wanted to emulate the bartender's behavior and add, "Sir," but refrained.

By the time Dwarka was ready to board the plane, Daddy had three doubles and was feeing tipsy. When it was announced on the PA system that passengers should board the plane, Daddy left the bar and joined Ma and Dwarka. Ma started crying, and dust got in Daddy's eye. Dwarka tried to calm Ma, while pretending not to notice Daddy wiping his eyes with a multi-colored handkerchief.

"Just one week, and then you gon have to come back and pick me up to take me home," he told Ma. Then he looked at Daddy. "Or if you busy, I can take a taxi."

"Whatever time, day or night, I gon come fuh you," Daddy told him.

Then Dwarka boarded the plane. As Ma and Daddy looked at the aircraft gracefully taking off, Daddy put his arm around Ma's shoulder to stop her trembling.

"I hope nothing go wrong with the plane," she told Daddy in a quavering voice.

"The plane gon go safe. You gon come back with me to pick Dwarka up next week?"

Ma looked at Daddy as if he was stupid to ask her such a question, but after a while, she simply said, "Yes!"

They stayed in the departure lounge until the plane disappeared in the sky, and then reluctantly left. Ma was still sobbing when they reached the parking lot, and Daddy opened the passenger side front door for her. As Daddy started the car, Ma told him in a rather shaky voice, "Leh we stop at Land of Canaan to see Buddy Deo."

Buddy Deo was Ma's eldest brother, who owned a substantial parcel of land, on which he planted rice. Land of Canaan was situated on the East Bank Road and most relatives dropped in at Deo whenever they returned from the airport. The meeting between Ma and her eldest brother was expectedly cordial, and Deo did not hesitate to send for a bottle of five-year-old El Dorado rum, and his wife, Aunty Bhani, immediately selected a chicken which would up in a pot with masala.

Ma, of course, did not sit with the men, but joined Aunty Bhani in the kitchen, where she helped her prepare the meal. Aunty Bhani liked to imbibe, and always kept a bottle in the kitchen. She and Ma had a few drinks while they were cooking, and Aunty Bhani, who liked to talk, kept Ma's thoughts occupied.

"Last night I see Major in me dreams," she told Ma. Major was Ma's father, and he had passed away the year before. "He look so real to me. Like he still alive."

"Daddy work so hard to look after all a we," Ma said. "I wish dat I can dream him."

"Sometime dream look so real," Aunty Bhani observed.

The two women talked in this manner until the meal was ready, and they took the rice and chicken curry upstairs to Daddy and Uncle Deo, who continued to drink as they ate. Ma and Aunty Bhani also took a few while they were eating in the kitchen.

By the time Ma and Daddy were ready to resume their journey home, only half of the sun was visible on the western horizon, but they were happy—Ma because she was able to visit her brother whom she hadn't seen for a long time, and Daddy because he was satiated with food and drinks. As they reached Prospect and turned in Cowboy Street, Ma became emotional again.

"I gon really miss Dwarka," she complained to Daddy. I so accustomed to see his face when I wake up in the morning." And she reached for the handkerchief in her handbag.

"He gon come back in one week," Daddy replied.

Daddy was approaching our house by then and stopped the car on the road just before the house, exited and opened the gate, before driving the car to its usual parking spot under the house. Then he and Ma walked up the stairs to the door. Daddy, who was quite intoxicated, fumbled in the pocket of his trousers for the house key, but the other knickknacks, including loose coins, in his pocket, combined with numerous drinks of El Dorado, caused him to fumble for quite a while. Ma, still emotional, was waiting impatiently.

Then the front door opened, and Ma and Daddy saw Dwarka staring at them. Ma dropped her handbag and Daddy, who always stuttered when he was angry, upset or surprised, opened his mouth and started making unintelligible sounds.

They stood there for a long time, looking at Dwarka as if they were seeing a ghost, until Dwarka asked them, "You all gon come in, or you gon stand there all day?"

"But..but…but…but…" was all Daddy could say, as he actually backed away a step.

Ma froze and kept staring at Dwarka, but could not utter a word.

When Dwarka put his arm on Daddy's shoulder, Daddy recoiled at first, but as soon as he realized that the hand was comprised of real flesh and blood, he relaxed.

"When the plane was in the air, the pilot realized that something was wrong with the engine, and decided to turn back," Dwarka explained. "They postponed the flight until tomorrow. You all come in." Dwarka felt awkward to invite his parents into their own house.

Ma became slightly unfrozen by then, and she and Daddy, kept giving Dwarka looks of disbelief, as they slowly entered the house. As Ma collapsed on one of the sofas, she regained her power of speech. "I glad that the pilot turn back and the plane didn't crash," she said, as Dwarka handed her a glass of water.

16 RAMLALL'S STRANGE COURTSHIP AND WEDDING

My uncle, Ramlall, lived about a mile west of where we lived in the village of Canal No. 2, and his courtship and wedding were much talked about in the village.

Twenty-three-year-old Ramlall, slim, and about five feet, ten inches tall, was very particular about his appearance. He was always clean-shaven, with his jet-black hair held in place by liberal amounts of brillantine. He made sure that he shaved every day and his black leather shoes were polished to a military shine, although he knew that the dust on sunny days and mud on rainy days would mask the shine.

Ramlall was a smart, handsome guy and was one of the few people in Canal who attended high school after completing the *Primary School Leaving Certificate*. Few people in our village continued their education after attaining this certificate—for several reasons. The high schools were located in Georgetown, the capital of Guyana, about twelve miles away from our residence. This necessitated travelling to Vreedenhoop by hire car on a brick road, crossing the Demerara River by ferry and then walking to the location of the high school. The other reason: while education in the primary school was free, students had to pay to go to a high school.

My grandfather had pulled Ramlall out of Wray High School after only three weeks, because he was offered a coveted job in the factory at Wales Estate. Before he left high school, however, he shared a phrase which according to him, was French. For months, we walked around the village, repeating, *La cuisiniere la repas is en la cuisine*, proud that we could speak French. I later learned that there is no French phrase like that, but nobody in our village disputed our assertions that we were speaking French.

Ramlall's job at Wales Estate was to ensure a constant temperature of the cane juice being boiled to make sugar. Because he was not required to be in the sugar cane fields, he was always neatly dressed, with a sharp crease in his trousers and his shirt carefully starched and pressed. He rode his shiny new Humber bicycle with a swagger to work every day because the estate truck, which transported workers to the sugar estate and back to our village, did not offer him the flexibility he desired. In addition, he did not want to mix with the workers who cut cane or were in the *weeding-gang*, whom he considered lower than himself.

Uncle Ramlall spent an inordinate amount of time washing and polishing his coveted bicycle, especially the spokes. He once saw the village postman riding his polished bicycle in the sun, and admired the way the spokes glittered as the wheels revolved. There and then, he made a promise to himself that the spokes in his bicycle would glitter the same way.

Between the sugar factory and his home lived the love of his life— a buxom girl named Sunita. Nineteen years old, Sunita was of medium height and had very fair skin. In the days when most people wanted to be like our English colonizers, fairness was considered extremely desirable. She had finished sixth standard in our local elementary school and had passed the *Primary School Leaving Certificate.* The next stage for her, according to the custom in our village, was to get married and raise a family.

The most outstanding feature of Sunita's anatomy were her prominent breasts She was doubtlessly aware of this, because she wore very tight blouses, which accentuated that part of her anatomy. She tied her long hair, which reached to her lower back, in a ponytail, and she liked to flip her ponytail over her shoulder and let it rest between her breasts. Often, she pulled the ponytail over her tight blouse, with predictable results.

Sunita waited every day under her house, which like all the houses in Canal, was built on posts, to get a glimpse of Ramlall, or for him to get a glimpse of her and her breasts. Often, Ramlall showed off by taking both hands off the handle of his bicycle and wave to her. For weeks, my uncle racked his brains in vain to find an excuse to stop and talk with Sunita. He had almost given up trying, when his bowels provided the solution just as he approached her home.

Sunita expected him to glance at her, raise his hand and ride on. Instead, he steered his bicycle towards her house and across the plank which served as a bridge across the four-foot drain, and rode straight under the house.

"Where you all latrine?" he said. "A strong shit hold me."

"The latrine deh fifty yards behind, along this path. Follow yuh nose," she added with a smile, as she gave him a page of *The Daily Chronicle*[21] to be used as toilet paper.

Ramlall leaned his bicycle against one of the posts of the house and hurried along the path, the single page of *The Daily Chronicle* clasped in his hand, while Sunita waited for his return. Her parents had not yet returned from the farm, and did not know of the attraction between her and Ramlall. She was excited because of Ramlall's nearness, but was nevertheless worried that her parents would come home and discover Ramlall in their yard.

If they come home, I will explain that he just come in to use our latrine, she rationalized. This relaxed her, and she thought: *Ramlall never see me so close.* She was glad that she had combed her hair and had put some Ponds powder on her face earlier that day.

When she saw Ramlall walking along the path between the coffee trees, he was looking much more relaxed. He had recently seen the film, *High School Confidential* and was attempting to affect the swagger he had admired in Russ Tamblyn, lamenting the fact that he did not have a sweater to throw over his shoulder. When Sunita pulled on her ponytail, Ramlall stopped walking—he was mesmerized. As he approached the bottom house, and went to the standpipe to wash his hands, he felt that he couldn't just jump on his bicycle and ride away, but had to say something to Sunita.

"You all latrine really stink," he observed.

Quick as a flash came her reply. "Na shit! It na must[22] stink!"

Ramlall was impressed by her wit, but couldn't come up with an excuse to linger any longer. However, he was satisfied that he had

---

[21] One of the two daily newspapers in the country; the other was *the Guiana Graphic.*
[22] The reason for it

found a reason to talk to his beloved, and slowly walked towards his bicycle. Before he rode off, he turned to look again at Sunita, who smiled encouragingly.

The next afternoon, the sun was shining brightly as Sunita took her favorite spot on a bench and waited for Ramlall to pass by her house. She was not surprised to see him steer his bicycle under the bottom-house again. She had a sheet of *The Chronicle* ready for him. Ramlall had wanted to go to the toilet after his shift at the factory, but decided to wait until he reached Sunita's house. He walked more leisurely than he did the previous day and decided to forego the swagger of Russ Tamblyn, as Sunita admired his immaculate turnout.

As he walked back from the latrine, my uncle wanted to talk to Sunita, and again, he couldn't think of anything to say. As soon as he was within earshot, he asked her, "Why your parents don't buy *Graphic?* It more soft than *Chronicle."*

Once again, he was impressed by Sunita's wit as she quipped, "I gon give you sand-paper next time."

Ramlall desperately wanted to continue the conversation, but again, was at a loss for words, so he reluctantly jumped on his bicycle and rode away. When he reached the main road, he glanced back to see Sunita and was pleased to notice that she was still looking at him. He raised his hand in farewell and felt that he was on cloud nine when she reciprocated.

This process continued for two weeks, and Ramlall looked forward to his trips to the latrine, until one day when the sky was overcast and it was threatening to rain, he rode under the house to find Sunita's father, Mangal, lying in the hammock. Mangal had gotten wind of the situation and decided to come home early from his farm, to protect his daughter's reputation. A thin, wiry man, with a large moustache, Mangal did not change from his work-clothes, which were covered with dust and sweat. He had not shaved for a week, and as he rose from his hammock, and wiped the sweat off his face, Ramlall felt intimidated, even though he was younger and stronger.

Mangal faced Ramlall, whose urge to go to the latrine somehow seemed less urgent. Mangal did not waste any words, as he looked Ramlall directly in the eyes and asked him, "You only want to go to the latrine when you reach the house Sunita live in. You gon marry she, or you gon shit somewhere else?"

Quite suddenly, Ramlall's bowels seemed at the point of releasing, and the only reply he could think of was, "I really got to go to the latrine," as he grabbed a sheet of *The Chronicle* lying on a chair and escaped along the dirt path.

As he squatted in the latrine, Ramlall had time to think about the situation. If the truth be told, he was glad that things were being brought to this point. He was completely captivated by Sunita and wanted to marry her, but was unsure how to proceed.

Ah gon tell him to speak to my big brother about it, he thought. *Since our father died, he act as father to all of us.*

When Ramlall approached the bottom house, Mangal was still standing, leaning against a house post, a Bristol cigarette hanging from his lips. Ramlall did not even look in his direction, but went directly to the standpipe and took his time to wash his hands. Then he glanced at the kitchen attached to the house and saw Sunita smiling seductively at him. This gave him some courage—he squared his shoulders and walked quickly to Mangal.

"You got to talk to my brother, Baba, and *ask for me*.[23]"

Mangal took this as a sign of consent. "All right! Tell Baba that I gon come on Saturday night and ask home for you. Sunita is a good girl. She can cook, and she learn sewing. She don't walk brazen like some a dem girl who don't have no shame. She down she head[24] when she walk."

And she got nice breasts too, Ramlall thought, as he jumped on his bicycle. This time, he didn't look back and he didn't mind the few drops of rain falling on him as he pedaled home.

**

---

[23] It was the custom for the parents of the girl to go to the home of the boy and propose marriage.
[24] Look down

The following Saturday evening, a half-moon was visible and there was enough light to see the outline of the trees when Ramlall walked across the bridge spanning the canal to our home. He had already acquainted my father with the situation and wanted to be there when Mangal arrived. Daddy had bought a bottle of XM five-year-old rum in preparation for Mangal's visit and Uncle Ramlall and Daddy decided to get a head start while they were waiting for his future father-in-law.

When Mangal arrived, Ramlall noticed that he had a close shave and had trimmed his moustache. He was also wearing a clean white shirt and blue serge trousers, with his hair neatly combed. He appeared much less threatening to Ramlall than when the two last met.

"You gon take a drink?" my father told Mangal as soon as he sat down.

"I does take a drink now and again, but I don't drink to get drunk," Mangal responded as he took the glass from my father. Daddy handed him the bottle, and he poured a tall drink and chaser. Directly after he finished the drink, Mangal turned to Daddy.

"I don't want to get drunk when I tell you this, but it look like me and you gon be family. Ramlall and Sunita like each other, and Ramlall tell me to come and ask for him to marry Sunita." Mangal then looked at Ramlall, who nodded.

"Ramlall tell me he agree. When you want to do the wedding?" Daddy replied as he reached for the bottle to pour another drink.

"Leh we see! It June now. Leh we plan the wedding fuh December," Mangal suggested.

This time, it was Ramlall who answered, "December good. Leh we do it in the first week of December, so that it don't interfere with Christmas."

Daddy knew his brother. *He want Sunita in his home for Christmas*, he thought.

"Okay! I gon tell my wife to prepare for the wedding the first week of December." Then, as Mangal reached for the bottle, he thought of something else he wanted to say. "You know how people like to talk and make up things. Every afternoon, Ramlall stop at my house to go to the latrine, and Sunita alone home. It don't look so good. It give my daughter a bad character. Can Ramlall go somewhere else until after the wedding?"

Ramlall thought it was a small concession to make, and before Daddy could say anything, he replied, "Okay! The factory got septic tank. I gon go there before I come home."

So Ramlall and Sunita reverted to their old ways of communicating, knowing that better days were ahead.

Daddy decided that the wedding would take place at our home and as the date approached, enough firewood was split for the open fires, over which large pots of rice were to be boiled and dholl, curried potatoes and other vegetables cooked. Leaves of water lilies were cut to serve as plates. Several of Ramlall's friends elected to be among the group which formed the *bariat*,[25] and contracted with the owners of cars to carry them to the bride's residence. The cars were carefully washed and polished and then decorated with colored ribbons.

When the long-awaited day arrived, Ramlall, dressed in a colorful *mowr*,[26] set out to Sunita's house in the car he had hired for this purpose. The members of the bariat had bought numerous bottles of rum which they drank as the cars, horns tooting loudly, followed the bridegroom. Ramlall had hired a group of *nagara*[27] musicians to accompany him. The music heralded his approach when the car in which he was riding stopped, and he walked regally to the bride's home, followed by members of his bariat, who danced frenziedly. Just as he crossed the plank across the four-foot drain, Ramlall was greeted by Mangal. As was the custom, Mangal washed the feet of his future son-in-law and asked him to take care of his daughter.

Then Ramlall was ushered to the *maroo*[28] where he sat on a low

25 People accompanying the bridegroom to the wedding, usually held at the bride's residence
26 Artificial crown. The bridegroom was considered king for this day.
27 A type of very lively music played at weddings
28 An area brightly decorated, where the wedding was performed.

bench. His friends continued drinking and ogling the girls, who were dressed in their finest outfits, some of whom responded with wide smiles.

Sunita arrived, her face covered with a thin veil and she sat on Ramlall's left, and the pundit chanted the sacred rites, before the couple was covered with a sheet. Sunita raised her veil and Ramlall applied the red sindhoor[29] on her forehead. Traditionally, this was when the bridegroom saw his bride for the first time. Then the couple walked around the sacred fire five times and the wedding was complete.

While all this was happening, some connections were made between the members of the bariat and the young women who were sitting in the tent or helping with the wedding activities. Some of these resulted in future weddings.

Finally, the pundit handed Ramlall the legal marriage papers. "You and Sunita only got to sign this, and we finish," he told Ramlall.

Ramlall hesitated for quite a while before he told the pundit in as casual a manner as he could muster, "You married us already. We gon sign the papers later."

Mangal, who thought that everything was going quite smoothly, was astonished. He stood up to his full length and threatened, "The gal ain't leaving this house if you don't sign the papers."

"But the pundit married us already," Ramlall countered.

"Sign the papers, or else the gal staying just heah," Mangal emphasized, as he jabbed his forefinger to the ground.

Ramlall thought of taking Mangal up on his word, but then he imagined the disappointment faced by his relatives and friends if he returned home without a bride to show for all their efforts. Realizing that he was outmaneuvered, he reluctantly took the pen from the pundit and signed the marriage papers. The pundit then handed the papers to Sunita, who signed them with a flourish. They would later be submitted to the Office of the Registrar General, in Georgetown,

---

[29] Coloured dye

104

to legalize the marriage.

When the wedding party returned to our home, the bride was accompanied by two *luknis*.[30] Usually, only one lukni was required, but for one reason or another, Sunita's mother felt that her daughter needed extra protection.

In the Hindu tradition, a marriage is not consummated until the second Sunday and a lukni is sent with the bride. The bride usually returned to her parents' home the following day and the groom would bring her home the next Sunday—referred to as *Second Sunday,* when the marriage was consummated.

When Ramlall returned to our home with his bride, almost all his friends who constituted the bariat were highly intoxicated. They had even managed to slip Ramlall some rum in a water coconut while the pundit was performing the marriage ceremony.

The usual rituals were performed, with my mother welcoming Sunita to our home. Then the luknis and Sunita retired to a bedroom, which was prepared by my mother and my sisters, and guests lined up to present money to the bride in order to *see*[31] her.

Ramlall, still peeved that he had lost the fight related to the signing of the legal papers, went downstairs, had quite a few drinks with his friends and relatives, and danced to the Hindi songs blasting on the juke box. The alcohol fueled his desire for Sunita, and determined to assert himself, he headed straight to the room where Sunita and the two Luknis were seated on the bed. Everybody who wanted to meet the bride had already done so and the room was empty, except for Sunita and the Luknis. Sunita looked even more beautiful and desirable in her wedding dress, which did not conceal her breasts.

His demure bride looked so ravishing that Ramlall's desire became even more intense. Emboldened by the numerous drinks he had consumed, he turned to one lukni. "You signed for the girl?" he

---

[30] Custodians who ensured the bride remained virtuous until she was officially brought to the groom's house on the Second Sunday.

[31] It was customary for invitees to present money to the bride in order to meet her.

asked.

The Lukni, unaware of where the conversation was going, retorted, "I didn't marry none girl. Why I gon sign for the girl?"

Satisfied with this answer, Ramlall turned to the other lukni and repeated the question.

The lukni was indignant. "How I gon sign? I can't read or write. My mother and father never send me to school, or else who gon do the house work?"

Ramlall was getting tired of all the verbiage. "You sign for the girl, *Yes or No?*"

"I can't write English, how I gon sign?" Then seeing that Ramlall was getting extremely red in the face, she simply said, "No!"

Ramlall, speaking louder this time, told both luknis, "If none of you sign fuh the girl, then get out. I sign fuh the girl." He practically pushed the luknis out of the room and bolted the door.

The conversation was heard by most of the people in the hall, in spite of the rather loud music. The men and some of the younger women were bemused, while some of the older women made *tutting* sounds.

One old woman with a white rumal and no teeth, muttered loudly enough so that those around her could hear, "He don't have no shame," as she got up and went downstairs to remove herself from the scene.

When the creaking of the bed was heard even above the loud music, my father tactfully went downstairs and turned the volume of the jukebox to the highest level.

Ramlall's courtship and wedding were the talk of the village for months, until Basdeo ran away with his uncle's wife, but that is another story.

PART II
STORIES FROM THE NEW WORLD

17 A DOCTOR, AN ACCOUNTANT, AND AN ECONOMIST AT DINNER

My niece, Sarojini, is a member of a very prosperous and ambitious family who lived in Georgetown, British Guiana, and each member of the family did everything within his or her power, including the cultivation of the right contacts to keep the prestige of the family intact. Her father was the headmaster of a primary school, and the entire family placed a tremendous value on education. Nobody was surprised when she married Kumar, an accountant and scion of a wealthy merchant family from Georgetown.

Sarojini and Kumar were well matched. Sarojini was of medium height, slim, and very fair, at a time when fairness was considered an asset because of our British rulers. She was one of the students chosen to attend Bishop's High School, because of her excellent performance at the Common Entrance Examinations. The government had used this examination as the basis for the placement of students in various secondary schools in the country and Bishop's High, which admitted only female students, was considered the best. The comparable high school for boys was Queen's college.

Kumar was a good-looking young man of twenty-five, with thick black hair and a neat moustache. In Guyana, he had lived with his prosperous family in a large white house in Camp Street, Georgetown. Kumar had attended university in London, England and had graduated with a CMIA degree.

When Guyana achieved its independence from England, the politics and election rigging by the Burnham dictatorship resulted in a mass exodus of Guyanese, mostly to America, Canada and England, and both my family and Sarojini and Kumar were a part of that exodus. Canada was our destination and we found ourselves living in Toronto or its suburbs. Our families were very close in Guyana and my niece and I continued to celebrate important occasions together in Toronto. Sarojini and Kumar did their best to accommodate their hard-drinking—some would say drunken— uncle at these get-togethers.

Very often, the evenings at Kumar's and Sarojini's home began with a nice quiet dinner, with wine. While I and most of the male invitees enjoyed the dinners, we all waited, not so patiently, for the after-dinner activities, when we progressed to scotch and soda. After a few drinks, Kumar usually went to the kitchen and brought an aluminum basin, which he placed upside-down on his lap. Then he turned to his often-invited brother-in-law, Partab, also a heavy drinker with a thick beard and melodious voice, and say, "Blow a tune, man."

Partab would burst into song, while Kumar drummed on the basin and others clapped to the tune. I can still remember when I was invited with Partab and a few others to a party at Sarojini's and Kumar's place. The evening commenced quietly and everybody enjoyed the food, drinks and good company. Then the ladies went upstairs. Kumar barely waited until they were at the head of the stairs when he dashed to the kitchen, brought an aluminum basin, and we started to sing.

The ladies took their time upstairs and we continued our singing. At about 2:00 a.m., we heard a loud knocking on the door and when Partab and I opened it, we saw two police officers, one male and one female, on the landing. They were dressed in heavy coats and seemed bored and slightly angry. The male officer had his right hand on the pistol in his hostler, and I remembered reading in the *Toronto Star* that many police officers were killed or injured while responding to domestic assaults or home disturbances. I was determined to reassure the officers that they were in a safe situation.

"Would you like a drink of something, officers?" I asked, as I turned to look at the half bottle of J&B Scotch whisky on the coffee table.

"No thanks! We came because your neighbor complained of the loud noise you are making," the female officer responded. "I realize that you can get carried away after a few drinks, but it's late, and your neighbors want to sleep. Keep it down! Okay?"

I noticed that the male officer kept looking past us at the bottle of J&B, and guessed that he wouldn't have minded a drink on that cold night.

"Sorry officers!" Kumar told them. "We will stop now."

"Okay! I hope so, because we have to give you a ticket if we have to come to your house again," the female officer warned.

The police turned to leave, after exhorting us not to drink and drive, but I couldn't help noticing that the male officer gave one last look at the bottle of Scotch, before he left to go to his patrol car.

Needless to say, the party ended in a somewhat glum note.

**

Near Christmas of 1984, I was helping Leila, my wife, to decorate our Christmas tree when the telephone rang. When I picked it up, I was pleased to hear Sarojini's voice.

"Uncle, I have an important dinner next week Saturday," she announced in a somewhat formal tone. "I am inviting you and Auntie, an economist, an accountant, and their wives. It's not a Partab type sport. I know that you are capable of attending a formal dinner. I want you to behave like a doctor." The last sentence referred to the fact that all my relatives were extremely proud of the fact that I had recently graduated with a Ph.D. in education.

"That's quite a dinner, you'll be having," I managed to say.

"Yes," Sarojini replied. "These are important people, and I've been boasting about you."

Suddenly, I became quite self-conscious. "What should I wear?"

"You don't have to wear a suit, but dress good," she said. Then she added as an afterthought, "None of that sweatpants and hoodie you always wear."

"You got it," I assured her.

On the day of the dinner, I put on a pair of brown trousers, my best dress shirt and a red and white sweater in recognition of the season. My wife, Leila, wanted to wear her sari, but I assured her that a nice dress would be adequate for the occasion.

As we stepped out of the house to go in our car sitting in the driveway, we noticed that it was quite cold and windy, and the dusting of snow on the streets was swirling around. When we were in Guyana, a warm tropical country, we enjoyed looking at photographs of the scenes like the one we were witnessing, on Christmas cards, but we didn't enjoy the cold, wind and snow as we drove to Sarojini.

Leila and I had an unspoken arrangement that I would drive to a party, and she would drive home. I will not insult the reader's intelligence by explaining the reason for this arrangement, but the falling snow did not cause me to experience any anxiety about her driving back, because we had driven to my niece's home many times.

When we knocked on the door of Sarojini's house located on the Markham, north of Highway 401, and she opened the door, I saw her ready to impress in a long dinner dress, and a sparkling necklace. Her hair was immaculately coiffured and adorned with some sparkling beads, and her face was carefully made up. I also noticed that her nails were manicured and I immediately regretted telling Leila not to wear her sari.

"The economist is already here," Sarojini told us with a smile. "Come and let me introduce you and Auntie."

After putting our coats in the closet, she led me and Leila to the living room to meet the economist, who got up and greeted me enthusiastically. "Dhanraj, I'm so glad to see you. I didn't see you since we met in Guyana. I heard that you were in Canada, but I didn't know how to contact you."

"Ramlall, how are you doing? I, too, heard that you were in Canada. How did you know my niece?"

"She was in one of my classes at the University of Guyana when I was lecturing there."

Before I left the university to join the Guyana Defence Force, Ramlall and I were in the same class in the University of Guyana, and had some memorable drinking bouts together. He was later hired as a lecturer at the university, while I joined the army as an officer. We started reminiscing about Guyana, about the university, and about the reasons for our leaving Guyana, until we were interrupted by the doorbell.

"That's the accountant," Sarojini observed as she gathered her dress and walked regally towards the door.

After hanging up the coats of the accountant and his wife, she ushered them into the living room, and started to make the introductions, but was surprised when he nudged her aside, and made a bee line towards me.

"Dhanraj," he shouted. "Man, I haven't seen you since you left Wales School to join the Guyana Defense Force. Everybody said that you forgot all about us."

"Nah, man. I was just busy. Nice to see you again, Gobin. How you know Sarojini?"

"Through her husband," he replied. "Kumar and I studied in England together."

"Those were nice times we had at the junior staff club," I reminded Gobin. "I didn't even know how to hold a billiard cue until you guys showed me. Now, I'm not such a bad player. Except when I have had too much to drink," I added.

Although his next remark was addressed to me, Gobin turned to the others in the living room, and laughing loudly, remarked, "I remember when you passed out leaning against the pool table."

"But that was after I made the winning shot," I reminded him.

Gobin did not reply, but sat beside me, and we continued to talk about the good times we had at Wales.

The evening commenced with very fine wine, poured in crystal glasses. As we sipped the wine, Kumar, Gobin, Ramlall and I looked at each other, each one of us knowing that the others were thinking that Scotch would be better, but restraining ourselves because Sarojini worked so hard to prepare for a sophisticated occasion. When Sarojini indicated that it was time for dinner and led the way to the dining table, I was astonished by the sparkling display. The silver cutlery was polished to a shine and there were two crystal glasses per person, one for water and one for wine. Blue embroidered napkins were neatly folded and placed on the table, but there were no plates.

When I looked quizzically at Sarojini, she whispered to me, "We will be served."

Sarojini went to one end of the table, while Kumar sat at the other end. "You sit at my right, and Auntie will sit beside you," she told me.

Then she assigned places to everyone and ensured that Gobin sat next to Kumar, so that they could reminisce about their experiences in England, while the lady hired by Sarojini to help and serve for the evening stood by the kitchen. When Sarojini indicated that we were ready to be served, she brought in the first course.

The cream of mushroom soup was served in deep China soup bowls, followed by a delicious salad of Romain lettuce, with tomatoes, mushroom and Caesar dressing. For the main course, we were served choice cuts of beef, along with baby potatoes and vegetables. Dessert—custard and gulab jamun—was the best part.

Sarojini had no need to showcase me to her guests, because they both knew me, but throughout dinner, she emphasized my role in the army, my stint as ADC to the President of Guyana, and of course my recently acquired Ph.D., as we all helped ourselves to the rich red wine. By then, I was no longer self-conscious. The wine, dinner, and Sarojini's boasting of my accomplishments served as fuel for my ego.

After dinner, the male guests retreated to the living room, wine glasses in hand, and Sarojini and the women went upstairs to the game room to talk about whatever women talk about in these situations.

"This wine is good," Gobin said, "but I can still feel the chill from the wind in my bones."

Kumar took the hint immediately. "You want something stronger?"

Although the question was addressed to Gobin, Ramlall and I answered in unison, "Yes! Scotch would be good."

Kumar extracted a forty-ounce bottle of Chivas Regal from the liquor cabinet and placed it on the coffee table.

"I'll go get glasses," he told us, as he left for the kitchen. When he returned with four crystal glasses, Gobin had already opened the bottle of Chivas.

"You guys will chase with water or soda?" Kumar asked us, as he placed the glasses on the coffee table.

"Soda!" we all replied.

We set aside our wine glasses, poured liberal amounts of Scotch with some soda and savored the drink as it burned its way down our throats. The first one was followed by a few more.

Then Kumar, his face flushed with alcohol, turned to me and uttered his famous inebriated words, "Blow a tune, man," as he left for the kitchen.

I needed no prompting. As soon as Kumar returned with an aluminum basin, I burst into a song which I had sung many times in my drinking bouts.

"Gal from Polder, come *doh doh*[32] pon me shoulder. Teacup and saucer, to give me loving water," as Kumar kept the rhythm on the basin and the others clapped.

Whether he was inspired by my singing, or whether he felt that he could do better, Gobin volunteered to sing the next song, followed by Ramlall. The singing continued, and as I clapped to keep time for Ramlall's song, I saw my niece walk down the stairs and look upon the group with displeasure, before she scowled and returned upstairs to join the ladies.

Being fortified with good Scotch—we were into our second bottle by this time—we ignored Sarojini and continued with our songs and loud drumming. None of us heard the knocking at the door and we were surprised when we saw Sarojini walk down the stairs to see who was knocking at that hour.. We stopped our singing and clapping in time to hear a loud and insistent voice outside the door.

---

[32] Sleep

"You all gon stop this noise, or you want me to call the police again?".

"That's my neighbor," Kumar explained. His face mirrored his alarm, as he immediately put his glass down, stood up, and made his way towards the door.

We all got up to accompany Kumar and were surprised at what we saw. Standing outside the door was a man with a long beard, a dressing gown over his pajamas, and a black coat over it all. A grey tuque was thrown carelessly over his head, and specks of snow were all over his tuque and outer clothing. He kept dusting snow from his coat as he spoke.

We were just in time to hear Sarojini placating him, "I'll speak to the men," she told him in a soothing voice, as she placed her hand on his forearm.

"I'm surprised that the walls of this house aren't thick enough to keep out the noise," Gobin offered by way of explanation.

Then he decided to throw a sop to Cerberus, and asked the neighbor, "Would you like a drink?"

"I want you to keep your noise down so that I can sleep," the neighbor snarled, as he turned away to return to his house.

As she closed the door, Sarojini looked at Kumar, then at Gobin and Ramlall, and finally thew a scorching glance at me. She was trying to figure out what to say to the company of professionals when she was interrupted by Leila, who spoke directly to me, "Dhanraj, you guys made enough noise. It's time for us to go home."

Quite contrite, I meekly nodded. As we put our coats on, and just before we walked out the door, Sarojini came up, and told me in a scathing tone, "I invited a doctor, an economist, and an accountant to a formal dinner. And look what happened!"

For a few moments, guilt rendered me speechless. Then emboldened by the immense amount of alcohol I had consumed, I muttered, "You invited people, not titles," before I allowed Leila to lead me to our car.

Just as we walked through the door, I heard Sarojini mutter to herself, "You can take them out of Guyana, but you can't take Guyana out of them."

Leila was silent for most of the way home, but just as we turned into our street, she told me, "Your relatives are very proud of you, but you have to behave like a doctor."

"I was never a doctor before, so I don't know how to behave like one."

I intuited that that was the wrong thing to say, but the alcohol I had consumed made me careless.

"You are a drunken rass," she concluded.

"Guilty as charged!"

By then she had turned into our driveway and I went straight to bed after we went into our home. Even in my drunken state, as I lay on the bed, I thought of how important it was to my niece to have a group of professionals in her home for an elaborate dinner. Although I did not accept sole responsibility, I regretted the part I played in transforming her sophisticated dinner into a drunken bout.

However, up to this day, I still cannot understand why Sarojini blamed me solely for how that evening turned out, and she showed me in many ways that she never forgave me.

It's been over thirty years since that memorable occasion and I have been invited to her house many times since the incident described above, but never to a formal dinner.

18 I'LL RAISE MY PRICE

At the time I was teaching co-operative education at the Scarborough Center for Alternative Studies (SCAS) with another teacher, Mary Patterson, my wife, Orna, and I were replacing the fifteen-year-old beige carpet in the upper story in our house. The dust from the carpet made my year-round allergies worse and we decided to sleep in the family room in our basement until all the work was finished.

A creature of habit, I always became very disoriented whenever my routine changed even slightly, and on the morning after the first night of our new sleeping arrangement—a Thursday, I forgot my wallet. It was usually on the dresser of our room, but I had placed it on my writing desk on the main floor when I vacated our bedroom. It contained my driver's license, my credit cards and some spending money. Luckily, I remembered my employee pass and the key to my office, which Orna had put on the breakfast table, and which were on a chain which I wore around my neck. I later blamed Orna for not putting my wallet in the same place.

SCAS was housed in a building attached to Centennial College, near Progress Ave. and Markham Road, and a long corridor connected the school with Centennial. The corridor facilitated access of staff and students of SCAS to the food court at Centennial. The proximity of the two establishments led many people, including educators, to come to the erroneous conclusion that SCAS was part of Centennial College. The school was, in fact, operating under the auspices of the Toronto District School Board..

I was teaching in the adult section of SCAS. The students in this section were mostly new immigrants, many of whom spoke languages other than English. After attending English as a Second Language classes, students focused on subjects like Accounting, Office Administration, and Computer Studies, which enabled them to access the job market. Many Canadian businesses strangely required *Canadian Experience* before hiring applicants. This was a problem for immigrants who complained, "How are we going to get *Canadian Experience* if nobody hires us?"

The co-op program was designed to provide this experience to students, and most students enrolled in this course, when they were ready to enter the workplace.

Classes at SCAS started at 8:30 a.m. and I arrived at around 7:50 a.m., so there was plenty of time to grab a coffee from the Tim Hortons outlet at Centennial. The co-op offices were in the basement of the school, and as I made my way to the main floor where the corridor was located, students and teachers were walking up the long ramp—SCAS prided itself in being accessible—leading to the main door, I felt lucky and honored to be a part of this establishment in my post-retirement years, because I worked with students who had held prominent positions in their home countries, and were required to make fresh starts in a new country. I shared my own struggles as an immigrant with them and acknowledged that they faced more challenges than I did, mostly because I had immigrated from Guyana—an English-speaking country.

As I went across the corridor and joined the rather long line at Tim Hortons, I reached for my wallet—I had the habit of having my money in my hand before I reached the counter, to save time. I frowned on people who ordered coffee or other items, and took what seemed like hours searching their pockets or purses for money. I pulled my hand out of my pocket, it came out empty, and I thanked God that I did not embarrass myself by ordering a coffee, and then discovering that I had forgotten my wallet.

I made my way back to the SCAS not overly concerned. I prided myself on my popularity and thought there would be no problem borrowing some money from one of my colleagues

My first mark was a teacher of English, Kim Wilson, with whom I was always bantering and with whom I struck up a friendship despite her business-like, no-nonsense manner and outspoken behavior. When I approached her, I noticed Kim was grading an assignment and her face was quite serious, bordering on a frown.

"Kim, I forgot my wallet at home this morning. Can you lend me ten dollars until tomorrow?" I asked the slim, tall blonde. I expected her to immediately reach into her purse and give me the money, but instead she gave me a no-nonsense look.

She replied, "The last person I lent money to quarreled with me when I asked her to repay the money, and I promised myself that I will not lend money to anyone again."

"You should have said 'The last person to whom I lent money,' not 'the last person I lent money to,'" I told her sullenly.

She responded to my correction of her language by quoting the words of Shakespeare, "Nether a borrower nor a lender be," as she continued reading the student's assignment.

I was taken aback by her refusal, but was still confident that I would be able to borrow a least ten dollars from one of my colleagues, and considered whom I should ask next.

My eyes focused on Ram, a teacher from Trinidad, who was sitting at his desk, reading a book, which was required for the course he was teaching. He looked up as I approached. I noticed that his eyes were bloodshot and knew that he had been drinking the previous night. Most teachers suspected that he had a problem with alcohol, but nobody voiced any concern.

"Ram, I am doing renovations in my home, and in the confusion I forgot my wallet," I told him. "Can you lend me ten dollars for coffee? I will pay you back tomorrow."

It seemed to me as if Ram's eyes became a few shades redder as he opened the drawer of his desk, took out two packets of instant coffee and offered them to me. "The kitchen has a kettle, and the fridge has milk. There is sugar in the cupboard. You can heat water and make a coffee."

"No thank you, Ram," I responded as I walked away, disappointed. Ram was still holding the packets of Nescafe in his outstretched hand when I was ten steps away.

As I made my way back to my office, I rationalized, *I can't really blame him. So many people in the streets asked me for a looney to buy a coffee, but I knew that they were going to buy cheap wine with the money they collect.*

I was resolved not to embarrass myself further, until I approached my office and saw Mary sitting in her office, which was adjacent to mine. Mary was originally hired at SCAS as a hair-dressing teacher, but had switched to co-op after she discovered that she had developed allergies to certain hair dressing products. She was slim, of medium height and with a beautiful face which always wore a smile. She had the bluest eyes I ever saw, but I could not determine the color of her hair because she changed the color monthly—each color complementing her natural beauty.

I should have asked her in the first place, I thought.

I pushed my head inside her office. "Mary, I am doing some renovations to my home, and I forgot my wallet. Can you lend me ten dollars until tomorrow?"

"Sure, Ken!" She opened her bag, fished out a crisp ten-dollar bill, and handed it to me.

"I promise to repay it tomorrow," I told her holding my right palm shoulder high, as I pocketed the ten dollars.

By then, my longing for a coffee fix had evaporated, but the ten dollars in my pocket gave me a sense of security. In the afternoon, although I did not badly need a coffee, I went to Tim Hortons and treated myself to a café-mocha and a honey cruller doughnut, just because I had the money to pay. As I enjoyed them, I promised myself that I would not forget my wallet the following day.

Mary and I were scheduled to monitor some students who were doing their co-op placements in the *Multicultural Community Interpreter Services*, MCIS for short, at 12:00 noon on the following day. In the morning, she was monitoring students at another location and I in another. We had agreed to meet in the MCIS office.

As I pulled into the parking lot at MCIS, I was pleasantly surprised to see an ex-soldier of the Guyana Defense Force (GDF), Grant Adams, who served in the platoon I had commanded. He was now the parking lot attendant. I had later resigned from the GDF as a captain, and Grant Adams left as a corporal. We hadn't seen each other in years, and happy that we reconnected, we spent some time reminiscing about our experiences in the GDF, and sharing about our activities in our adopted country. I explained the reason for my presence in MCIS, before leaving to meet with the students and their supervisors in the office, but I had neglected to mention Mary, my colleague.

Mary later joined me, the supervisors and three students in the office, where we had a productive discussion about the students' progress. Placements at the MCIS were enviable because most of our students spoke a variety of languages and were encouraged to perceive the fact that they spoke multiple languages as an asset in the multicultural, multilingual city of Toronto. Many students who did their placements at MCIS were later hired as translators, and others were hired by banks and other businesses which needed multilingual employees.

Mary and I often treated the supervisors of our co-op students to lunch as a token of our appreciation for hosting the students. In this case, the supervisor, Amily, a vivacious lady of about forty, who spoke seven languages, decided to meet us at a restaurant located about fifteen minutes away. Mary and I decided it would be better to go with my car, then return to the MCIS parking lot and pick up her car, before returning to SCAS. I still remember the curious look on Grant Adams's face as I escorted the gorgeous lady to my vehicle.

It was mid-October, and an unusually warm, sunny day. We knew we did not have many more warm days to come and Mary decided to take advantage of it. She wore a low-necked, sleeveless, blue flowered dress which reached just above her knees. The neck of her dress revealed the curvature of her ample breasts, which the brown silk scarf that was thrown over her shoulder did little to conceal. Always a beautiful woman, on that particular day, she looked ravishing.

Grant gawked as I opened the passenger side door for Mary and we took off for lunch. We met Amily at an *all you can eat* Pakistani restaurant and took our time savoring the dishes. I ate so much, that I knew that I would be unable to eat dinner that day. After lunch, Amily had to go to her bank before returning to her office and Mary and I emphasized to her how much the students enjoyed doing their co-op placements at her office, before we decided to head back to MCIS to retrieve Mary's car.

I was wondering why Grant Adams was giving me a wide-eyed

look as I returned to the parking lot, but decided to ignore it, parked, and went to the passenger side to open the door for Mary, who always teased me about how much she enjoyed having doors opened for her whenever she was being driven by me.

It was only when Mary exited the car that I remembered the ten dollars I had borrowed from her. I knew I was very forgetful and I also knew Mary would not ask me for the money she had lent me, so I was determined to repay my debt before I forgot it entirely.

"Mary, that ten dollars you lent me, I better repay you now," I told her, as I reached for my wallet.

"Not here! Not now!" she almost screamed.

"But if I don't give you the money now, I know that I will forget," I insisted.

"Not here! Not now!" Mary repeated, waving her arms frantically.

I happened to glance at Grant Adams whose mouth was open and whose eyes were almost out of their sockets, but I can be stubborn at times, and kept on insisting that Mary take the money. By then two other people in the parking lot had their eyes on us, and Mary, who obviously didn't want to prolong the scene, reluctantly accepted the ten dollars and placed it in her purse, before going to her car.

On my way out of the lot, I handed Grant Adams five dollars along with the parking ticket.

"Ten dollars!" he exclaimed.

"But the sign says five dollars for the whole day."

"Five dollars for parking. But whatever that gorgeous lady did must have been worth more than ten dollars. No wonder that she didn't want to take it. With all due respect, Captain, I didn't know that you were so cheap."

I started to give him an explanation, but thought better of it and decided to leave him to ponder the mystery, as I handed him five dollars for parking. Driving on Highway 401 on my return to SCAS, it finally dawned on me why Mary made such a fuss about accepting her own money, and realized that I owed her an apology.

When I reached SCAS, I popped my head in her office. "I'm sorry that I was so stubborn, Mary. I now realize why you didn't want to take the ten dollars in the parking lot. That ex-soldier was surprised that I was offering you only ten dollars, and thought that you didn't want to take the money because you expected more for services rendered."

Mary flashed her blue eyes at me and grinned wickedly. "I'll raise my price," she told me, before she refocused on her computer screen.

19 SAVED BY A COMMA

On a snowy Thursday morning, we were sitting in the office of the English department in Bowside High School when Bob Singer, his face contorted with frustration, looked up from his desk and addressed his colleagues. I always felt inadequate in Bob's company, and on that day, I felt even more self-conscious. My blue jeans, old brown sweater and sneakers made a sharp contrast to his starched and ironed Calvin Klein shirt, blue silk tie, pin-stripe suit, and shoes polished to a military shine.

"I've got to teach these Grade Eleven students how to use the comma," Bob told us. "Look at these two essays. Elaine put a comma after every phrase, and Mike used only three commas in his entire essay."

Bob held up the two essays which were filled with his penciled comments, for all of us to see. Disappointment showed on his face when none of us got up from our chairs to read the students' assignments.

However, he perked up when another teacher, Sam Bahadur, tall and lanky with shoulder-length hair, who had immigrated from Guyana like I did some years earlier, started to speak.

"The comma is extremely important," Sam emphasized. "Last summer, I went to New York, and a comma, really the absence of one, saved my brother in Guyana from getting a bad name."

All the teachers directed their attention to Sam, as they leaned back in their chairs and smiled. All of us recognized that Sam had a story to tell about almost everything, and although we were busy, and classes were due to start in fifteen minutes, we took a break from our preparation to hear Sam's story, because his accounts were always very detailed and interesting. In many cases, they were also instructive.

Dressed in black trousers, white shirt, and a red and blue striped tie, with black moccasins, Sam clasped his fingers and put his hand around his stomach, before recounting his experiences. He ran his fingers over his thick black beard before he recounted his summer adventure.

Last summer, my wife and I made our first trip to New York since we immigrated to Toronto, I hadn't seen my sister and brother, both younger than I, since they immigrated to New York. My sister, Kamla, and her family live in Queens, while my brother, Balram, and his family resided in the Bronx.

I had known Kamla's husband, Ramraj, before he started courting my sister, because he was working in the office at Diamond Sugar Estate, and I was teaching in the primary school in Grove. Of course, we became closer when he frequently visited our home in Windsor Forest on his Honda motorcycle.

My elder brother, Abel, and I were heavy drinkers although we were still in our teens, and we took Ramraj to the local rum shops, although Kamla had warned us that Ramraj was not much of a drinker, and she didn't want him to "become like us." It seemed as if there was no danger of Ramraj becoming like us—whenever we went to one of the watering holes in the village, he would mix a few drops of rum with almost a quarter bottle of Pepsi, and we would tease him that he was drinking most of our chasers.

Two years after he and my sister were married, Ramraj left Guyana to study accounting in the U.S., and decided to stay in that country. Kamla joined him later, and their two daughters and son were born the U.S. Ramraj was proud to tell anybody who would listen that his children were American citizens by BIRTH. I was surprised to learn that he was drinking quite heavily in the United States, and I often felt guilty that our drinking bouts in Windsor Forest might have encouraged him.

Balram joined them in U.S. the following year, and got married to Beatrice, a nurse, who sponsored him as a resident. They settled in the Bronx, where they raised three fine sons.

Sam took a sip from the red mug on his desk, which was half-filled with coffee before he continued his story.

Everybody in our family knew that Ramraj was an emotional person, and I deduced from his many late-night phone calls, that he was becoming even more so, especially after he had had a few drinks.

I was anxious to see my siblings and their families and arranged a flight through *The Last-Minute Club* so that my family and I could visit them. The airline with which we flew had declared bankruptcy between the time it flew us to JFK Airport, and the time we were scheduled to return to Toronto, but that's another story.

Kamla, who was born two years after me, and dressed immaculately in a pink sari and colorful sandals, met us at JFK Airport at about two in the afternoon, and drove us in her blue Toyota Corolla to her home in Queens. As we drove along the highway, I found myself looking forward to eating her chapatis and a variety of curried vegetables because, as a vegetarian, Kamla cooked and ate no meat. However, the variety of vegetables she cooked ensured that she and her family ate a balanced diet.

When we arrived at her large, two story-home, with a spacious verandah in front, I was surprised to see Ramraj standing in front of the gate of the wrought iron fence with a roll of carpet under his arm. He was below average height, and he seemed to have shrunk a few inches since I last saw him. He had a full head of white hair, and his face was covered with a few days' worth of stubble.

Why the carpet under his arm on a hot, summer day? I asked myself.

"Ramraj is waiting for you. You go first," Kamla nudged me as she spoke, and I preceded her. As soon as we entered the gate, Ramraj rolled out the carpet with a flair. I then noticed that it was bright red, and realized that my brother-in-law was literally giving us the red-carpet treatment.

"Welcome to my home in the UNITED STATES," he said. Then he started crying as I walked up to him and hugged him. He refused to let go of me until Kamla intervened.

"Sam, everybody gone in the house, and Balram and Beatrice

126

waiting for you. You got to come in now. Ramraj gets emotional and starts to cry because of any little thing."

I disengaged myself, and followed my sister into the house, with Ramraj trailing. He had left the red carpet on the concrete strip as a reminder of his colorful welcome to us. My brother, Balram, and his wife, Beatrice, were standing inside the house, impatiently waiting for us to join them. Apparently, Ramraj had requested them to leave him alone, so that he could welcome us in his dramatic way.

Balram, younger than I by six years, was about five feet, nine inches tall, and quite slim. Quite smart, Balram was a teacher in Guyana, and had graduated from the University of Guyana with a B.A. before he immigrated. In the U.S., he was working in the communications department in Bell Telephone. Beatrice, his wife, was a nurse in the local hospital.

After greeting my brother and his wife, the first thing that caught my eye was the welcome sight of a half-gallon bottle of Chivas Regal sitting majestically on the coffee table, and surrounded by crystal glasses. Ramraj had previously justified his excessive drinking to me by arguing that he always drank cheap whisky, but had obviously made an exception for my visit.

He had stopped crying by this time, and proudly instructed me: *Sam, you take the maiden.*

I happily obliged, and Balram, Ramraj, and I settled down to enjoy the fine Scotch. We finished almost half of the bottle, and stubbornly ignored Kamla's consistent exhortations to *come and eat something.*

After the third time, Ramraj suggested, "Why don't you bring us something to act as cutters? We will snack as we drink."

Then he turned to me and Balram, and offered his expert advice. "When you eat too much, you become bloated, and you can't drink any more. When you drink and eat a little bit of cutters now and again, you can drink the whole day."

Both Balram and I nodded as we poured another drink. A few minutes later, Kamla brought a plate of pakoras, potato balls, and mango sauce which she placed on the coffee table. We reveled in each other's company as we snacked, drank, shared jokes, and reminisced about the good times we had in Windsor Forest. The more I drank, the more I missed Abel, older than I by eighteen months, and I regretted thar he was unable to get visas for himself and family to come to either Canada or the U.S. Abel and I were very close and had many adventures together in Guyana.

I couldn't help telling Ramraj and Balram, "I wish Abel were here. I really miss him. He would have really enjoyed this," as I pointed to the bottle of Chivas Regal.

I was not surprised when Ramraj put his glass on the coffee table, looked at me and started crying. I attempted to console him.

"Ramraj, Abel, you and I had some good times, in Guyana. I know that you miss him, but we'll meet up again some time."

"You, Abel and me were so close." Ramraj held up his right hand, and placed his index finger on top of his middle finger. "I never imagined that Abel wanted me to die."

"Why would he want that?" I quickly countered. "We had such good times in Guyana, and I know that Abel likes and respects you very much. Except when you drank all of our chasers," I quipped.

"I have it in writing," Ramraj said between sobs. "I kept the letter, because I know that nobody will believe me. I gon go and get it for you," he continued as he walked up the stairs. He was still crying as he made his way to his room, and Balram and I looked at each other in disbelief.

Ramraj returned with a letter, and pointed to the underlined part. Abel had written: *Ramraj, that bastard didn't die yet. If he doesn't die soon, I may die of vexation.*

"You see? What more proof do you want?' he asked us.

My mind was numbed by numerous drinks of Chivas Regal, and I still tell myself that I am a good reader, and had I been completely sober, I would have picked up the meaning of the sentence immediately. I held the letter, and thought of my brother. *Abel likes our brother-in-law. Why would he write this?*

Another excuse I still make to myself for not reading the letter accurately, was that Ramraj had set me up as a reader to anticipate the fact that Abel wanted him dead. I read the letter with that mind-set.

I was numbed by what I had just read, and not knowing how to respond, I showed the letter to Balram. He looked at the underlined parts, threw a *school-master's* look at me, then turned to Ramraj.

"You ever heard of the noun in apposition?"

"How you gon explain what Abel wrote?"

Balram leaned towards Ramraj, "Did you ever ask Abel if the President wasn't dead yet?"

"Everybody want the President dead," Ramraj responded. "Since he became president of Guyana, he thieving money and ruining the country. And he ban everything. You can't get flour to make roti. No wonder everybody leaving the country."

"Well, Abel responded to your query—*Ramraj, that bastard didn't die yet. If he doesn't die soon, I may die of vexation.*

He didn't want to name the President because had somebody opened the letter, he could have been in trouble. But he did NOT put a comma after *bastard*, so that means that he is referring to somebody else. Had he written *Ramraj, that bastard, didn't die yet*, then he would have meant you. The extra comma meant that the term *that bastard* would be a noun in apposition, and would have referred to you."

I could almost hear Ramraj's brain churning as he took the letter from Balram and began to study it. I prided myself that I picked up on Balram's explanation immediately, and I decided that I would not be outdone by him.

"The comma after *Ramraj* means that he is addressing you," I said looking at Balram who was nodding. "*That bastard*, is referring to the President."

Ramraj, his face contorted with concentration, looked at the letter for quite a few minutes, and then his entire body shook so much as he sobbed, that I had to pry his glass from his hand and put it on the coffee table to prevent his drink from spilling.

"I blamed Abel all these years for nothing," Ramraj said, through his tears.

I looked at him crying hysterically, then glanced at Balram who looked as proud as a peacock that he was able to resolve the miscommunication,

Then I picked up my glass, and mumbled in my Chivas, "Saved by a comma."

**

Sam Bahadur smiled as he completed his story, and we all sighed with relief that the story ended well.

"Bob, go and teach your students how important it is to use the comma correctly," Sam advised.

Just then the buzzer sounded, indicating that it was time for classes to start, but before he left the staffroom, Bob turned to Sam, "Sam, can I use your story to demonstrate to my students the importance of punctuation?"

Sam nodded, and we all gathered our folders and hurried to our classes, while contemplating the importance of a single comma.

20 MY APPRENTICESHIP WITH THE MAN WHO TAUGHT YOUNG CANADA

O ur world is full of unrecognized and unsung heroes. Even though the obituary of Dr. John McInnes was headlined, *The Man Who Taught Young Canada to Read*, and focused on Dr. McInnes' professional achievements, I feel that Dr. McInnes was not sufficiently acknowledged as a kind, compassionate, and basically a decent human being. I hope that a description of my apprenticeship with him will help readers to see him in that light, as well as a consummate professional.

In 1975, I was a recent immigrant to Canada, and I had graduated from the University of Guyana with a B.A. degree, with a major in English Literature. I was aware that my search for a teaching job would have a better chance of success if I could show some Canadian qualifications, and in 1976, I enrolled in a B.A. Honors course at York University where I met Beverley Vilyakainen, who was taking the same course in Canadian Literature. Beverley was about thirty-eight, with blond hair which she kept shoulder-length. Later, I discovered that she was very spiritual, and did yoga and meditation exercises regularly. She was also a firm believer of naturopathy and kept her visits to traditional doctors to a minimum. Most likely, these activities were largely responsible for her youthful and slim figure, and her energetic personality.

I shared with her that I was a teacher in Guyana and that the Ontario Ministry of Education had issued me with a *Letter of Standing*, based on my degree from the University of Guyana and my attendance at the Government Training College—the only teachers' training college in Guyana at that time. The *Letter of Standing* entitled me to teach in Ontario, but I found it difficult to get a job, even as a supply teacher, because I had no contacts.

Beverley looked at me intensely with her grey eyes, and advised,

"An honors degree in English will definitely help you in your job quest. But if you're looking for contacts in the field of education, the best institution in which to be studying is the Ontario Institute for Studies in Education. We call it OISE for short. It is full of teachers, administrators, and supervisory officers studying for their Master's and PhD degrees. When are you graduating?"

"If I continue with my Honors degree, I will graduate in two years, but I can graduate with an ordinary BA this June."

"Why don't I bring you an application for admission to OISE, and you can submit it? If you are accepted, you can graduate with a BA and then continue your studies at OISE. Believe me, if you are looking for a teaching job, your time will be better spent in an institution where you can pursue your Master's degree, AND network with a community of educators."

I accepted Beverley's advice, submitted the application for admission to OISE and was accepted into the M.Ed. program, with a focus on curriculum. OISE, located at Bloor and Spadina Avenues, was considered the best institution for educational studies at that time and I was elated to be accepted, although I was not currently teaching.

I was interested in reading instruction, and I elected to attend some preliminary courses in the teaching of reading. The very next summer after I was accepted to OISE, I decided to take a course in reading and it was my good fortune to meet Dr. John McInnes, who was considered the leading instructor in reading in OISE.

Dr. McInnes was a kind man with a welcoming smile and sparse grey hair on his head. He insisted on being called *John* and valued each of his students, although his classes were packed because he was so popular. John taught his classes in the same manner he advised teachers to teach their students and respected the participation of all his students, regardless of whether they matched his philosophy or not. In addition, he had the knack of making each student feel special.

I remember one occasion when I contributed to a discussion in his class about students liking the sounds of words, regardless of their meaning. During coffee break, I was sitting alone at a table because

I had not yet established rapport with any of the other students, drinking coffee and eating a blueberry muffin. John left the table, where he was sitting with a group of students, walked over to me, and told me, "I want you to know that I appreciate your contribution in class."

I sat a little straighter as I stammered, "Thank you. I enjoy your class very much, and I am learning a lot."

That incident reinforced the fact that a few kind words can make and immense difference in a person's life. The opposite is also true. An unkind word or deed can scar a person for life. It would have taken only a few minutes for John to approach me, but those few minutes made the remainder of his summer course so much more enjoyable for me.

In the fall, I took another course with John, during which I expressed my interest in the type of instruction children who speak the Creole dialect received in reading. At that time, John was also the chief editor of Nelsons Canada, a publisher of children's books and he was immediately interested. After the class, he asked me to accompany him to his office.

"What are you going to do after your Master's degree?" he asked me.

"I am still looking for a teaching job, and I hope to get one soon."

"A teaching job would be nice," he responded. "You know that a large number of creole dialect speaking students are in our school system, and many of them are not succeeding. We need to find out why. You expressed an interest in these students earlier. How do you feel about enrolling in the PhD course? You can do your thesis on how these students cope in the reading situation. I earnestly want to produce books to which these students can relate."

"I am awed at how articulate the students in your class are," I responded. "I never went to a high school, and I took a Wolsey Hall correspondence course to achieve my *General Certificate in Education* at the Ordinary and Advanced levels. These are equivalent to Grades Twelve and Thirteen. All I had to do was read the notes, and regurgitate the information in the exams. I was not required to even know how to pronounce the words, only how to spell them. Even when I went to the University of Guyana, we did not participate a great deal in class. We listened to the lecturers, read profusely, and wrote the necessary papers and exams."

John chuckled. "You may not have spoken a great deal in class, but whenever you spoke, you always had something valuable to say." Then he tapped his head, "I know that you were always participating in here. And judging by your papers, you write very well."

"Very often, people have more confidence in me than I have in myself," I admitted. "If you think that I have the ability to complete the PhD program, I will apply to be enrolled in it."

John shepherded me through the Ph.D. program with the same patience, kindness, and understanding he had demonstrated in his classes. Frequently, I told my admired professor, "John, I know that you are well off, and don't need anything from me. But I promise you that many students will benefit from your kindness."

I have focused on the assistance I received from John as a student, but of course he supported a number of other students. For example, I learned that during the time I was at OISE, there was a Ph.D. student from Thailand who was planning to return home without finishing her degree because she ran out of money. John, who was quite successful financially and lived in the exclusive area of Rosedale, gave her enough money to continue her program and another professor, Dr. Jim Cummins, type-edited her thesis. I imagined her successfully returning to her home country and her proud family with a Ph.D. degree because of the intervention of two caring professors.

John also demonstrated his respect for people in his everyday life. When he visited my home for a curry and roti dinner, he had a conversation with my mother. John spoke perfect Standard English, and my mother spoke perfect Creole. I was fascinated as I listened to them, because they understood each other perfectly and there was absolutely no condescension on John's part.

For my doctoral thesis, I audio-taped, transcribed and analyzed a number of reading sessions involving Creole dialect-speaking students, and outlined strategies, related to reading instruction and reading materials, to increase the chances of success of these students. The oral defense of my thesis went well and I graduated with a Ph.D., thanks to John, who moved on to help other students.

Unfortunately, Dr. McInnes passed away in March 2008 and the world lost a great man, but his legacy would live on for a long time in the form of the books he edited, and the people he nurtured as educators. I am confident that these educators will maintain his legacy in assisting learners in our school system, and in our marvelous society.

Eventually I was hired as a teacher in the East York Board of Education and although I endeavored to emulate John's behavior, I was aware that I frequently failed. Despite my failures, I earnestly hope that I managed to repay some of the debt I owed this remarkable man.

ABOUT THE AUTHOR

Ken Ramphal was born in Canal No. 2 Polder in Guyana. He was a teacher before he joined the Guyana Defense Force as an officer cadet, and rose to the rank of captain. Ken was the ADC to the acting Governor General, Sir Edward Luckhoo and the President, His Excellency Arthur Chung, before he immigrated to Canada in 1975. Ken holds a B.A from the University of Guyana and a Ph.D from the University of Toronto. He was a teacher, an anti-racist Consultant in the East York Board of Education, and an Education Officer in the Ontario Ministry of Education. He is currently retired, and is the author of six books, including one, which he co-wrote with his sister and brother. He has also published several articles in educational journals. His book *Slippery Ochro* won 3rd prize at the Guyana Prize For Literature (fiction) 2023.

ALSO FROM MIDDLEROAD PUBLISHERS

MiddleRoad | Publishers

www.middleroadpublishers.ca

Making Literature See The Light Of Day

**All books available at amazon worldwide
ebook versions available from all ebook channels**

A TIME TO LOVE AN A TIME TO DIE
By Michael Joll
Finely drawn characters. Visually dramatic, tense and emotionally satisfying, this is one of the finest novels of the Great War. In this poignant story, the writing stands in stark contrast with the unvarnished brutality of trench warfare.

DANCING MY WAY TO 80
By Doris Naraine
Biography published privately and not available for sale.

ATTITUDE
By Dave Moores
Fresh, gritty and laced with dry humour, Attitude is a fast-paced story readers of all ages won't want to put down. It's dead of winter and an outbreak of weird stuff, random acts of vandalism are unsettling the citizens of Southmead.

DOWN INDEPENDENCE BOULEVARD AND OTHER STORIES
by Ken Puddicombe
"A brilliant collection of stories telling

137

the tales of people forced to leave their homes…craving the past, escaping from racial conflicts and dictatorship…" — Judith Kopacsi Gelberger, author of *Heroes Don't Cry*.

GABRIELLE
By Michael Joll
Gabrielle transcends time and space, taking the reader on a journey to Poland, France, Holland and Israel as she searches for her identity.

GENERATIONS
Biography published privately and not available for sale.

I WENT TO THE END OF THE RAINBOW
by Pramita Chakraborty
A beautifully illustrated, captivating tale about a young child who can't sleep and embarks on a adventure through the colours of the rainbow.

JUNTA
By Ken Puddicombe
"A gripping story (of) an imperfect democracy…the tension…builds increasingly from page to page." — Rico Downer, author of *There Once Was a Little England*

LOVE HAS TWO MOONS
By Franklin Mohan
With humour, insight and sensitivity, Franklin Mohan peels back the subtle layers of prejudice and racism in North American and Caribbean society — Raymond Holmes, author of *Witnesses and other short stories*

MEET ME AT THE FOUR CORNERS
Anthology
Twenty-six stories, fiction and non-Fiction, some of them prize winning

submissions from the writers of the Brampton Writers' Guild, are featured in this collection.

PEOPLE OF GUYANA
By Ian McDonald and Peter Jailall

"These beautifully crafted poems are shaped by their generosity of spirit and abundant capacity for empathy and fun…" —Clem Seecharan

PERFECT EXECUTION AND OTHER STORIES
by Michael Joll

"Michael Joll is a master of surprise endings, but they never seem forced. He always stays true to his characters and their worlds." —Nancy Kay Clark, author and editor, *CommuterLit.com*

PERSONS OF INTEREST
By Michael Joll

"Exotic and intriguing! Joll brilliantly captures the reader's interest with vivid imagery and a relentless sleuth." —Phyllis Humby, short story writer, poet and novelist.

POEMS FOR MARY
By Ian Mc Donald

"The garden which my wife has created, it is as much a work of art as a painting by a master spirit or a piece of perfect music by a composer." —Ian Mc Donald, author, poet.

RACING WITH THE RAIN
By Ken Puddicombe

"Puddicombe's brilliant novel…an historic political conflict in Guyana, during the Cold War and the cold cynicism and tragic irony of a state sacrificed to superpower hegemony." -Frank Birbalsingh, author of *Novels and The Nation: Essays in Canadian*

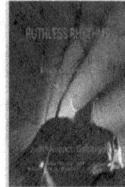

RUTHLESS RHYTHMS
By Judith Gelberger

If poetry is a window into the soul of the author, Judith Gelberger has opened one which illuminates some of the most painful emotions and experiences of human existence...—Raymond Holmes – Author of *Witnesses And Other Short Stories*

SCALING NEW HEIGHTS
Anthology

Forty-two pieces from the members of Pakaraima Writers Group are featured in this their first collection of poetry and non-fiction travel articles

TASTE MY WORDS

By Lisa Freemantle

Freemantle's compositions are imbued with a highly poetic energy instilling in the reader a subtle, penetrating fever of contentment...." —Dr. Franklin Mohan, author *Love Has Two Moons and Other Stories*

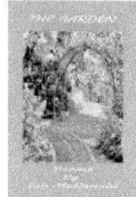

THE GARDEN
By Ian McDonald

Ian McDonald's poems are full of light and love. His easy style about the beauty of nature connects with his readers.

UNFATHOMABLE AND OTHER POEMS
by Ken Puddicombe

These poems cover a variety of themes, all connected to a childhood growing up in British Guiana, the rise of nationalism and the pre- and post-independence eras.

WEALTH THROUGH REAL ESTATE INVESTING
By Jay Brijpaul

Jay Brijpaul has tapped his vast experience and expertise in the Real Estate industry. This book provides comprehensive coverage of What, How, When, Where to invest in real estate.

WINDWARD LEGS
By Dave Moores

A pungent cocktail of choppy romance, corporate larceny and the thrills and spills of sailboat racing, Windward Legs is the rousing and captivating story of a woman's journey to rediscover who she is.

WITNESSES
By Raymond Holmes

"Suspenseful, historical, futuristic and riveting...stories and characters who will stay with you." —Bruce A. Hanson, Award winning author of adult and children's fiction.

www.ingramcontent.com/pod-product-compliance
Lightning Source LLC
Chambersburg PA
CBHW051245170626
46809CB00004B/1499